W9-DCD-638

NATIONAL DEFENSE

NATIONAL DEFENSE

A NOVEL

John A. Vikara

iUniverse, Inc.
New York Lincoln Shanghai

National Defense

iUniverse books may be ordered through booksellers or by contacting:

iUniverse
2021 Pine Lake Road, Suite 100
Lincoln, NE 68512
www.iuniverse.com
1-800-Authors (1-800-288-4677)

This is a work of fiction. All of the characters, names, incidents, organizations and dialogue in this novel are either the products of the author's imagination or are used fictitiously.

ISBN-13: 978-0-595-39098-4 (pbk)
ISBN-13: 978-0-595-83487-7 (ebk)
ISBN-10: 0-595-39098-6 (pbk)
ISBN-10: 0-595-83487-6 (ebk)

Printed in the United States of America

To those who served.

CHAPTER ONE

We passed a peace demonstration on our way to the airport. There were fires burning in fifty-five-gallon drums, and they cast a surreal glow over the street corner. It was as though the devil had come to visit and had turned over the streets of New York to the mobs, for their use whenever they saw fit. Pete and Johnny were silent as we skirted the area in my Mustang. I turned down side streets and tried to avoid any confrontation or even eye contact with any of the demonstrators. I didn't know what kind of spark would set off either of the foster brothers, particularly Pete. We had left the funeral home well after the official closing time of the last day of his mother's wake and were on our way to pick up Red Janek from La Guardia.

I parked the Mustang in the airport lot, and we waited for the traffic light at the pedestrian crosswalk to change. In our younger days—well before we had turned into thirty-year-olds—we may have weaved and danced around and behind the herd of cars and yellow cabs as though avoiding the bulls at Pamplona. But now we waited, part of the gathering crowd of travelers with suitcases and shoulder bags. The distant whine of turbo engines was barely audible over the sounds of the vehicles whizzing by us.

It was a humid night, still and windless. A slight glaze of perspiration covered my face, and I looked to see if my two old friends were affected by the sultry weather. We still wore the dark suit pants and white dress shirts that were part of the proper attire for the wake, but we had discarded our jackets and ties in the trunk of my Mustang. The brothers both looked fine, and I took a minute to study them as we waited. Johnny was six foot one and towered over Pete like they were a Mutt and Jeff duo. They called themselves brothers, but it was obvious it was not by birth. Johnny had a thin face with high cheekbones, a sharp nose, and short brown hair. Pete's face was round with an upturned nose, and he had longer dirty blond hair combed straight back. Their demeanors were different as well. Johnny was the quiet diplomat who kept his emotions in check. Pete was prone to outbreaks of rage and obsession when provoked. I smiled in reverence for them and once more vowed to do anything for them that would track down their mother's killer.

The green lens flicked on, and we followed the crowd to the sidewalk outside the bright lights of the main terminal. Lighted signs mounted perpendicular to the building advertised the different airlines operating at the facility. We side-stepped around redcaps and passengers moving into and out of the building and through groups of baggage carts or individual pieces of luggage along the side-walk. Idling cabs at the curb spewed exhaust fumes into the air, and the choking odor hung in the still air. We found the American Airlines sign and entered the building. The fumes and din of engines disappeared behind the doors and cool-ness of the air-conditioned atrium.

My sweaty face dried in the cool atmosphere as we weaved through the clamor of an unusually large late night crowd. We found the flight information board and watched as the several lines flickered like the numerals on a continually changing digital clock.

"Gate sixteen," I said.

"Yeah," Pete agreed. "His flight's on time. We still have twenty minutes before it lands."

"Let's grab a beer," Johnny suggested.

We sauntered along the fading maroon carpeting that led to the open front of the airport lounge and slid onto the high-back, dark vinyl cushioned stools. There were several customers, some with carry-on luggage at their feet, downing their liquid courage for a pending flight or celebrating their successful arrival. They sat along the length of the gold-swirled ebony bar. The red and blue lights that showcased liquor bottles on stacks of glass shelves reflected off the mirror behind the illumination and danced along the drink glasses in different patterns as the drinks were lifted or tilted or placed on the bar.

The bartender was about our age and wore a white shirt, black bow tie, and green vest. He took our order with a smile and nod of his head.

"It'll be good to see Red again," I said.

"Yeah," Johnny agreed. "What is it, a couple of years?"

"Yes." I lifted the tapered glass of draft beer that had been placed in front of me. "Here's to Red becoming a lieutenant. Image him an officer. He used to thumb his nose at authority when we were kids; now he's telling others what to do."

"The army knows a good man when it sees him. Two tours in Vietnam and a bronze star," Johnny said. He took a swallow of his beer. "That's officer material."

We silently sipped our beers for a minute until Pete said, "Too bad he's not here for pleasure."

I had avoided saying anything about Madge Wilson's death after we had left the funeral home, and Johnny had suppressed his feelings as well. It would be bad enough at the funeral tomorrow without hashing it over the night before.

"He's a good friend to want to be here for us," Johnny said. "That's what counts now."

"And what he'll help us take care of," Pete said.

"What do you mean?" I asked.

"Nothing, Jim," Johnny said as he patted Pete's shoulder. "Just that, uh, Red will help us get some info we need."

I didn't understand what he meant and let it drop. They both went back to silently drinking their beers. I glanced in the mirror and compared my features with Johnny's. *We* looked more like brothers, I thought. He was a little taller than me, but we had the same facial appearance and the same shade of blue eyes. He had been like a brother to me when we were growing up, before Madge Wilson adopted him and saved him from being kicked around foster homes and relying on the streets and his friends for any kind of comfort.

Johnny and his new foster brother had become inseparable, with Madge Wilson as the bond. Her sons were members of the criminal element of our old teenage gang, and Madge Wilson was an executive in the restaurant and catering chain owned by one of the connected relatives of the local crew. I wasn't involved in any of their business, preferring to stay straight, but I still maintained a strong closeness that had grown from our youth into adulthood. I had never felt any animosity toward Pete for moving ahead of me on Johnny's list. I was happy to have them both as good friends.

There was shouting in the terminal, and as it grew closer, the words became distinct. It was still another group of demonstrators that were constantly prowling the city. They appeared outside the lounge. There were five of them—three males and two females—strolling along the concourse and shouting their opposition to the war.

"End the war now!" one of the bearded males shouted. He broke away from his group and held out a flyer to us. "Support the peace movement."

"How would you like that thing shoved up your ass?" Pete said as he spun in his chair and tried to stand.

Johnny put his arm across Pete's chair and grasped the opposite arm. "Never mind them."

"Get lost," I told the hippie.

The hippie smirked and offered the flyer to the other lounge patrons. Most of the older crowd turned away and ignored him. A woman two seats from us took the flyer and glanced at it before laying it on the bar. He bowed to her and left.

The bartender brought us another round. "I see you feel like I do about them," he said as he wiped a spot on the bar in front of us with a white cloth. "I was over there. Marines. The sons of bitches used to send us cans of dog food with notes telling us to 'eat hardy, animals.'"

"They aren't all like that," the woman who took the flyer said. She was a few years older than us and wore a gray flannel suit-dress. "Most of them truly want peace and justice for our country."

"Oh, yeah?" Pete said. "Well, how would you like it if they killed your mother? What would you think of them then?"

"Well, I…" She stared at Pete for a moment. "Whose mother was killed?"

"Mine!" he shouted. "They blew her up with one of their stinking bombs."

"Enough," Johnny said. "Let's go." He stood and spun Pete around in his seat.

Pete stood. "I'm sorry, Johnny," he said. "It's just…I don't know if I can make it through tomorrow."

"You'll be fine," Johnny said. He slid a ten-dollar bill out of a silver money clip and placed it on the bar. "Keep the change."

"Thanks, buddy," the bartender said. "Good luck to you."

We started along the maroon carpet and I thought I heard the woman say she was sorry. The intense overhead florescent lights were a harsh contrast to the mood lighting of the lounge. Pete seemed to spring back from his episode and walked straight and smartly alongside Johnny.

Pete had been like a rock for the last five days. He deserved a slip or two. His position in assorted racketeering activities had made him a formidable, hard-nosed adult with the ability to withstand most anything thrown in his path. But as much as he tried to hide it, he had never lost that inner boyish good heart and emotion that kept him from being a common thug. He would weather this great emotional breakdown and continue his life, even with a chunk taken out of it. And all of us would help him do just that.

As we crossed the well-populated concourse toward the arrival area, I let my thoughts drift off. Five days earlier, Madge Wilson had been supervising the arrangements of a political affair at one of her company's catering halls when a bomb exploded in the ballroom outside the kitchen area. Madge had just entered the kitchen to check the preparations. She was the only one killed. It had been a small bomb triggered by some left-wing radical group no one had ever heard of before. I wasn't even sure if Johnny or Pete were told their name. The incident was one of many bombings that added to the dangerous atmosphere of the time.

It just seemed to me that responsibility was becoming a thing of the past. I still took my responsibilities to our country to heart. My father had been in World War II, and I had served for four years, discharged at the outbreak of Vietnam. Since I was never in combat, I didn't feel I had the right to criticize people not wanting to jeopardize their life, but—damn it—they shouldn't make it difficult for those who are there. The troops need our support; they don't need some spoiled, whiney little creep burning his draft card or some Marxist professor telling his vulnerable students why our country is so terrible.

Sometimes I thought I was just jealous of this new generation: their actions—whether peaceful or violent—were respected because of what many considered a righteous cause, whereas for those of us who had grown up in the previous decade, it had been illegal to gather in groups of more than three. But we were now adults with jobs and no free time to voice our own opinions. We did what we had to, engrained with the work ethics of our previous generations, while the streets of our city that were once our playgrounds were now being used for politics, handed over to mobs by acquiescing politicians.

We reached Gate 16 in the American Airlines terminal. About half of the fifty or so blue plastic and chrome chairs facing the white check-in counter were occupied. A dark-haired woman in a white blouse with a logo of double red and blue *A*'s over the left breast pocket stood behind the counter. Her head was bowed as she performed some administrative duty. The walls of the open area were decorated with travel posters of domestic and foreign locales. The florescent lighting overwhelmed the room and stressed the blackness beyond the large panoramic windows that looked out onto the flight line. The distant red landing lights of an aircraft passed through the darkness in a descent from the top corner of the far window to the lower corner of the last window before the wall. I wondered if that was Red's flight landing. We decided to stand and waited along the wall near the check-in counter. The dark-haired woman smiled at us, then returned to her work.

I hadn't noticed them when we had first entered the room. They were hidden from the entry view by the wall of an alcove on the other side of the room near a vacant ticket counter. And they were quiet, unlike our first encounter. The males wore baggy, flowered shirts and grimy dungarees. The one from the lounge and another had scraggly beards, and one was clean-shaven. The females wore over-sized sloppy dresses and had daisy chains in their hair. All wore sandals without socks.

I glanced at Pete and saw that he had seen them as well. He glared at them for a long minute before Johnny saw what was happening and ushered Pete to the windows. I followed and looked through the glass at the tow vehicles and baggage trailers springing into action below. I could see Pete's eyes in the window's reflection, staring hatefully at the reflection of the hippies. *Come on, Red. Hurry up so we can get the hell out of here.*

I tried to lose myself in thought, to make the waiting time disappear. I thought about Red, and the military, and found myself at my usual obsessive nagging doubts about my own courage. I had never had my mettle tested while in the service. There were constant alerts and threats during the four years—the Berlin Wall, Laos, and Cuba—but only threats. How would I have handled myself? I had been lucky to scrape by with no major incidents before the military, when I was a kid. I always tried to be a stand-up guy, and I knew I was seen in that light because of my friends' acceptance of me, but I always felt a little shallow like there was more I had to prove. Maybe my ego was trying to overpower—or just convince—my conscience to get that proof. The conflict would drive me nuts when I was alone with my thoughts. It would pry into my contemplation even when I tried to sleep and then follow me into my dreams.

I would keep telling myself that I had chosen to lead my current lifestyle because it was suited to my makeup. I wasn't a tough guy. I wasn't a hood. I was John Q. Public and always would be. But I was two months shy of thirty-one and my youth was fading and the nagging continued. Maybe I was having an early midlife crisis. Maybe I was just a fool, but I wondered if I was worthy of friendship with guys who had proven themselves many times in many ways, Red as a soldier, Johnny and Pete by their dark and sometimes dangerous illegal activities.

Then Red showed up.

I saw the uniform before I recognized Red Janek. I stared at the two rows of colorful ribbons, the Combat Infantry Badge and paratrooper wings, envious that I had never accumulated such trophies. Johnny and Pete moved through the line of passengers to welcome him. I came out of my delusions of grandeur and joined their smiling faces. We greeted Red, and he smiled and dropped his B4 bag so he could shake the multiple outstretched hands. His once bushy hair was now orange fuzz along the sides of his service cap. He was as tall as Johnny, and as I studied him I saw a more mature, determined face since our last meeting. Age lines had replaced most of his childhood freckles. We were all getting older.

"Jeez. The Wilson Brothers and Jimmy Yadenik, the three musketeers," Red said. "What are you two guys doing here?" he asked Johnny and Pete. "Shouldn't you be…?"

"The funeral home is closed for the night," Johnny said. "Everything's ready for tomorrow. We just had to get away from there for a little while. Seeing you again is good medicine."

"Baby killer!" The bearded hippie from the lounge leaped in front of Red and jerked his head like a pecking chicken. He spit and it oozed off the ribbons on Red's uniform.

Pete's fist smashed into the bearded face, and the pursed lips seemed to freeze in a fixed expression as the hippie sailed past his stunned friends. He struck the marble floor and slid on his backside before he rammed into the empty ticket counter. He crumpled into a ball and fell still. The woman behind the check-in counter screamed, and most of the people that had been sitting on the blue chairs or finding loved ones scattered toward the windows. Some of the chairs toppled and bounced along the floor.

The two females rushed to their injured companion and screamed when they saw his condition. One stayed to give comfort while the other sprang from her crouched position and rushed us.

"You beast," she screeched. "You've broken his jaw." She pushed past her two passive male friends. "You dirty warmongers." She leaped at Pete, her fingers curled like talons.

Pete sidestepped her. Johnny turned with a bullfighter's flare as she passed and grabbed her waist, spun her full circle, and let her loose. Her sandals flew from her feet and went the opposite direction from her hurtling body. She struck the two males as they braced to catch her, and they all slammed into an advertisement poster on the wall just behind them.

Red and I stepped to either side of Johnny and Pete, ready for retaliation.

"You cockroaches want trouble?" Pete shouted, pointing at the stunned group.

"Leave us alone, man," the bearded hippie still standing said. "We don't want any trouble."

"Then what the hell did you start for?" Pete made a move toward them, but Johnny held him back.

"Your friend, there," the clean-shaven one said, gesturing toward Red, "he's an officer. We're obligated to call people's attention to the fact that he and his ilk order the death and destruction of the downtrodden Vietnamese people."

"Were you obligated to blow up the building my mother was in, you piece of shit?" Pete broke free for a moment, his fists waving a few feet from the clean-shaven one before Johnny corralled him again.

"It wasn't them," Johnny shouted as he tightened his grip. "They're just punks who won't fight back. They're not worth it. We'll be seeing the real ones sooner or later."

None of the longhairs challenged the insult, not even the feisty female who had retreated to help her injured friend but still continued to leer at us in quick glances.

Pete's body seemed to shrink as he exhaled and dropped his hands to his side. He turned, and I thought I saw a mist clouding his eyes as he draped his arm over Red's shoulder and led him toward the black-ribbed surface exit ramp. Red had wiped the yellow saliva from his uniform with his handkerchief and tossed the God-knows-what-contamination into a silver trashcan.

I waited until Johnny turned. He gave me a wink, and I lifted Red's bag and fell in step but continued to stare down the group. The clean-shaven one followed us with his eyes, and I saw the animosity in their gaze. I made my stare as telling, and I had a strange sensation that we would hear about this guy again.

We had been too involved in our scuffle to have noticed but now saw that the crowd had moved back away from the windows. Some had formed a line along our path toward the exit ramp and applauded Red as he passed them. Others were silent with icy frowns. We marched up the ramp, leaving behind a murmur that became raised voices, soon to grow into shouting matches between the factions. Passions had been ignited, passions of disagreement that had been tearing apart our country for six years over a seemingly endless war.

CHAPTER TWO

The foster brothers had requested that the funeral be private. There was no other family; Johnny was a long-ago orphan and Pete never knew his father or any relative other than his mother. Only friends attended, and Madge and her boys had many friends. Most had paid their respects at the three-day wake, and only a selected number attended the gravesite funeral. It was easy to keep out the curiosity seekers, the authorities, and the press at a private funeral home, but not in an open, public cemetery.

Sure enough, the press was there for their scoop on this woman, the one killed by a radical organization's bomb, discovered to have been a top executive in a restaurant chain owned by a mob figure. They waited beyond the parked hearse, the flower car, three limousines, and assorted luxury cars that had constituted the procession, a little closer than the men with the binoculars and the walkie-talkies at the stone walls and open wrought-iron gates.

The gravesite was four plots from one of the narrow roads that divided the grassy sections of Calvary Cemetery. A hundred yards away, the superstructure of the elevated Brooklyn-Queens Expressway resembled a roller coaster, but its surface was flat and not programmed to plunge or evoke screams to disturb the peace of the surroundings, and when the priest's eulogy ended, only the sounds of the roadway hummed gently through the silence. The fresh scent of the multitude of flower arrangements around the gravesite, combined with newly cut grass, was overpowering to the senses. I heard someone sneeze three times, someone probably afflicted with allergies.

I stood in the third row of the invited group. It was a bit of a thrill and yet scary to be in the same congregation as people who haved had their names and pictures appear in the newspapers, but I was as much a part of Johnny's and Pete's lives as were the men they and their mother worked for. There were some who weren't celebrities and whom I knew well, such as Red, Sonny Krause, Crazy Lenny, and the Looney brothers, all of whom I had grown up with. Some had become local bosses, like Kelly and his cousin, Benny, once leaders of our teenage gang. Yes, the Vandals, friends and comrades of my youth, most having graduated from the classroom of the streets to lucrative criminal pursuits, that old gang of mine, *had* grown up.

Johnny placed his rose on the mahogany casket and bowed his head for a minute before stepping back to allow Pete to move into position. Pete slowly lowered to one knee and laid the stem of his rose across that of his brother's. He looked up for an instant before bowing his head again and saying, "We will always love you, and those that have done this will pay. My brother and I will see to it." No one gasped at the vengeful words because they echoed the thoughts of everyone there, whether the means of revenge were legal or otherwise.

Pete stood, and Johnny moved up to place his arm around his brother's shoulders. Heads bowed, they both turned and walked toward the lead limousine. A dozen or so of the waiting vultures began running toward them. Lenny and a squad of our guys intercepted the press corps before they reached the third limo and body-blocked as many of the group as they could. One of the reporters and his photographer evaded the line and got within shouting distance of Johnny and Pete.

"Isn't it true that your mother worked for gangsters?" the reporter asked. "And you two as well?"

Johnny and Pete looked toward the inquisitor. Their expressions must have been what the photographer wanted. He raised his camera and the shutter began clicking.

"How do we know that the explosion wasn't caused by some rival mob?" the reporter continued. "Why blame the SDS or the Weathermen or whatever other peace group for what may have been brought on by your mother's boss? Or maybe someone was seeking revenge against you two."

Yeah, I recognized the guy now. I had seen his picture a few times. He was from some really left-wing paper that was always sympathetic to the radicals. I started toward the reporter. "Why don't you get a job with the *Daily Worker*?" I shouted. "The Commie rag would welcome you with open arms."

He smiled sardonically, and the photographer swung his camera toward me. *Oh shit!* I heard the shutter click before I could duck away. Damn, I could see the caption: *Gangster's pal attacks press*, or something similar. It was guilt by association, just like when we were kids and were stopped by the cops. If you were with one of the so-and-so gang, then you were a so-and-so member, whether you really were or weren't. I hadn't done anything illegal since I was a teenager, but would that matter now?

I turned back and saw Lenny reach the pair. He swiped at the camera. *Get 'em, man. Break that damn thing.* The photographer pulled the camera from Lenny's grasp and tucked it into his body like a football. The press team turned to run just as our guys, other reporters, and a police car with a flashing red light spilled onto the scene. Johnny and Pete had entered one of the limousines in the chaos, and it was heading for the exit gate. At least I had given them the time to duck out and they would be spared any more anguish from these bastards. I was suddenly happy about not following up on my childhood ambitions of studying journalism.

I melted into the crowd of mourners, now drifting toward the parked cars. The celebrities, which the shutterbugs would've loved to shoot, were surrounded by their entourages and whisked to the remaining limousines to be hidden behind dark-tinted windows. I located Red and Sonny and we found our ride. Luckily, there was an exit gate that was for cemetery maintenance vehicles only and was not being patrolled by the NYPD, FBI, or whatever official organization was interested in the guest list of Mrs. Wilson's funeral. Since I was either on the cusp or already pegged as being part of the inner circle of a criminal empire, I figured why not show up for the after-funeral meal. What more trouble could I get into?

CHAPTER THREE

Johnny and Pete were still tense from the events of the day and invited a small group of us to unwind at a neighborhood bar following the official gathering. The press boys hadn't found the location of the restaurant, even though it was owned by yet another relative of Kelly and Benny and could've been traced with some minor investigation, and the afternoon went well. By now they were filing their stories or yelling "Stop the presses," or whatever they do at the editorial office. We could spend the evening in peace.

It was relaxing, so much easier to be with the regular guys instead of trying to act proper in front of elite strangers. Kick back. You're among friends.

We had pushed two tables together in the rear area of the narrow one-room tavern we had frequented since before we could legally drink. Swirls of cigarette smoke hung above the tables, and the multicolored lights of the silent jukebox against the wall behind us flickered occasionally from a short circuit. Pete sat at the head of the tables, and Johnny, Lenny, and Sonny Kraus were to his right. Red was in civvies. He and I sat along the other side of the unmatched table surfaces. Three partially drained pitchers of beer and a bottle of Johnny Walker Black sat among the assortment of glasses, chrome Zippo lighters, cigarette packs, and ashtrays. Puddles of liquid dotted the brown Formica surfaces.

"Here's to Mom," Pete said as he raised a glass of beer.

"To Mom." Johnny clinked his glass to Pete's, took a swallow, and then squeezed Pete's shoulder. "Let it go for now. We'll get even."

"I won't rest until it happens."

I saw Pete's misty eyes for the second time that day and felt tightness in my chest. I stood to hide my own emotions and turned toward the men's room. Red crushed out a filtered cigarette in one of the ashtrays and followed me. I held the door for him. "It's kind of crowded, but I'll share it with you," I said.

"No, go ahead. I'll wait 'til you're done."

The room *was* small, with only space for the bowl and a small sink. I completed my business, washed my hands, and then brushed passed Red at the door.

"When are you heading back to camp?" I asked as I stepped out.

"As soon as this deal goes down," Red said as the door swung closed.

Deal? What deal? I reached for the knob. *Stop.* Let him do what he's in there for.

As I returned to my seat, I heard Lenny say, "Only then will we let you hit the bastard." He looked up at me and fell silent. A cigarette hung from his lips and the smoke floated into his unflinching, piercing dark eyes.

"What's up?" I asked as I sat.

"Did you hear what I just said?" Lenny asked, the cigarette bouncing between his lips as he spoke.

"No, of course not."

Lenny's eyes narrowed. He pulled the cigarette from his lips. "Don't fuck with me, Jimmy. Did you hear what was said?"

"If I did, I forgot it."

Lenny turned to Johnny and tilted his head, requesting my dismissal.

"We didn't come here to discuss that," Johnny said. "Jimmy's here because he's a friend, and we're here to relax."

"But somebody might slip." Lenny tilted his head again. "We need to talk about a couple of things and he shouldn't hear them."

"Jim, we have some business to discuss," Johnny said. "Would you mind sitting at the bar for a couple of minutes?"

I stood obediently. "No problem." The end of the bar closest to the tables was empty. I sat on a cushioned stool and ordered a Coke.

I was used to being excluded from conversations when hanging with Johnny's group. They didn't want me to know their business, both for my protection and because they knew I wanted no part of it.

I exchanged greetings with a guy named Jack, who was just leaving. I knew him from around the neighborhood and also had met him at a couple of rallies for a new independent political party. The established parties seemed to have forgotten about the working-class people and small business owners. One took care of the rich and big business, the other the poor and big labor organizations and gave a platform to the loudmouth left-wingers. So who wound up paying the bills? The rich, big business, and big labor had their loopholes; the lefties found ways not to pay taxes, and the poor were…well, poor. There was just too much crap being shoved down the average guy's throat. A generation or two ago *we* were the poor, and now it wouldn't be long before the middle class again faded back into nonexistence.

I turned back to my group and began to analyze how they each fit into this business being discussed. What about Red? He had nothing to do with their organization. His new gang was the army, and it had been for the last twelve years. Why did he mention a deal? What about Sonny, the ex-con and body-builder? He's only been out a month. He's taking a chance of violating his parole just for being seen with some of these guys. And then there was "Crazy" Lenny, the hard case, with his scary pointed face that resembled a shark ready to chew into someone. He was the only one who belonged in the picture.

I turned forward as the bartender placed my Coke on a cardboard coaster. A dollar bill flipped on the bar from behind. "On me," Pete said. "You want a shot of rum in that?"

"No. Time to ease up. I have work tomorrow."

"Yeah, I usually would, too, but Johnny and I took a few days off." Pete gripped my shoulder. "Look, don't feel left out, buddy. You're still our best friend."

"Yeah, I know. Don't worry about it."

"Johnny and I appreciate your help with the funeral arrangements and all the running around you did for us."

"It's the least I could do. I'm honored for being invited to this special gathering." I pointed to the other four huddled around the table. "I mean, not even Kelly or Benny or any big shots. Just us six."

"You are special, my man. And that's why we never want to involve you in our things."

"That was fine before, but this is something different, isn't it?"

"I can't say anything, Jim."

"You're going after the scumbags that killed your mother, aren't you? Well, all bets are off. You know you can count on me to help."

"I thought you didn't hear anything." Pete's face froze in a grimace. "Didn't you tell that to Lenny?"

I stared into Pete's angry eyes and for a moment thought he was serious. "Up yours, man."

Pete's stone face cracked into a wide smile. He slung his arm around my shoulders. "Damn, I can't even test you anymore."

"Yeah, and you still have that great stare. But really, if there's anything, anything at all I can do…"

"Johnny and I know that, but you're here tonight because you're a good decent person, and it's exactly the reason why you're not getting involved."

"Oh, man, don't make me sound like a cream puff."

"Stop." Pete held up an index finger. "There's more to it than getting the bastards. Enough said."

"OK. But if there's anything, no matter how minimal…"

"We will definitely let you know."

"Thanks."

CHAPTER FOUR

Well, if I wanted to test my balls, it would have to be now, before whatever was going down went down. And it would have to start with the equivalent of teasing a rattlesnake. I wasn't sure whether it was that internal struggle or my true desire to help my friends, but whatever the reason, it was something I suddenly felt I had to do, and an opportunity had now presented itself.

The night was over; the bar closed early, and everyone had either driven away or hitched a ride. The humidity had given way to a cool night breeze. I was pulling from the curb when I saw Lenny swing open the driver's door of his black Cadillac and jump into the street.

"What's up?" I asked as I pulled even with him.

"Ah, this damn thing won't start. I've been having trouble with the starter."

"Try it in the morning." I reached over and flipped open the lock button on the passenger door of my car. "I'll give you a ride."

"Nah. Ain't you an auto claims adjuster? You should know something about getting it started."

"Yeah, an adjuster, not a mechanic. Besides, I'm tired. I wanna catch some sleep before dawn. Come on. Lock it up. You can bring somebody back tomorrow to get it going."

"Yeah, I guess so. OK." Lenny flipped away his cigarette butt, slammed the Cadillac door shut, and twisted the key in the lock, then slid into the seat next to me. "Shit, I ain't used to sitting on cloth seats," he said half-seriously.

"Sorry. Maybe when I become a vice president, I'll buy a luxury car and park my ass on leather. Are you still living at the same apartment house in Jackson Heights?"

"Yeah. On Polk Avenue." Lenny flexed his arms and smoothed the sides of his dark hair. "So why the hell don't you come to work for us and scam the insurance companies so you *can* drive a luxury car?"

"Because I'm happy driving a Mustang."

"I can't believe you wanna be a sucker for the rest of your life when you don't have to."

I didn't have a good reason that he would understand, so we were silent for the rest of the short trip until I worked up my courage. Lenny looked like he was beginning to doze, his pointy nose aimed at the floor. "I might be interested in this new caper," I said.

"Caper?" Lenny's head jerked off his chest. "What the hell is a caper?"

"This deal to get the bastards that killed Johnny and Pete's mother."

"What?" Lenny twisted in his seat and glared at me. "How did you find out?"

"Johnny and Pete are my buddies." I shook my outstretched index finger. "But don't think they said anything. I picked up things here and there, from their innuendos and when I visit the club. I put two and two together. Seeing Red and Sonny tonight, you know, it looks like the clan is gathering. So when you banished me from the table, I figured something was up." I took a deep breath and hoped Pete would forgive me for the lie. "When Pete came over to me at the bar, I put it to him, and he let a few things slip."

"Get lost," Lenny sneered. "Pete knows better than to say anything." He pointed. "Turn here."

"Maybe so, but I kind of conned it out of him. You know, he had a few too many and he was kind of vulnerable after the funeral." I double-parked in front of Lenny's building. "And he said he'd talk to Johnny about letting me in."

"So what'd he tell you?"

"How they know who the hippie bastards are that killed his mother and how Red is going to use his military connections to help out."

"Shit!" Lenny opened the passenger door and slid out. "I better tell Kelly. Nobody is supposed to know except the seven guys involved."

There had been only five at the table. I pressed on. "Don't tell me Kelly and Benny are gonna come down from their ivory towers and get their hands dirty."

"No, I'm looking out for their interests," Lenny said, leaning back into the open window. "Me, Sonny, and the Looney brothers. We're gonna make sure of the financial end of the deal."

Financial? "Yeah, sure. Pete didn't tell me about the Loonies. So I guess I'll be number eight?"

"You?" Lenny leaned his head back and his gaping mouth let out a stuttering laugh. "Not in a million years."

"Think again." I slowly slid the shift indicator into drive. "I didn't know a damn thing until now. I was only guessing. And it all started when you told me to leave the table. You opened the door by asking if I had heard what you said. What do you think Kelly and Benny will say when they find out you spilled the deal to someone? And I have five witnesses."

"You fuckin'…"

I stomped on the gas pedal and Lenny spun free of the car. I only heard the beginning of his shout: "You're dead, you mother…"

CHAPTER FIVE

She was a strong, proud, beautiful woman. I almost thought girl, because of her youthful appearance, which resembled a petite, ponytailed teenager rather than a woman one year shy of that dreadful barrier of thirty years old. Her dancer's body provided the poise that was the deciding physical sign of maturity. I loved her so much, but, like most couples who had systematically extended their engagement for five years, we had our differences. Gwen stood in the archway between the living room and kitchen of our small railroad-style Greenwich Village apartment. She waited until I had slugged a drink of soda and placed the bottle back in the refrigerator.

"I should label that bottle as private so no one else will get your germs," she said.

"I thought that was a given. I mean, that this is mine and the vegetable juice concoction is yours."

"Something a lot healthier than that poison."

"Agreed, but so what?"

"The point is that maybe a guest would like a drink of that soda."

"So how would they know if I drank from it?" I closed the fridge door. "You don't have to tell them."

Gwen twisted her face in disgust. "That's terrible."

"Besides, the only *guests* we get are your showbiz pals. I thought the only thing they liked was stuff made behind the iron curtain."

"Let's not start that nonsense again." Gwen stiffened her back. "Just because they're against that hideous war doesn't mean they're communists."

"Then why do they support communist organizations? Why do they march with scumbags carrying North Vietnamese and Vietcong flags?"

"Anyone who's against the war is free to demonstrate."

"So that means that because I don't like how the war is being conducted then I can march with them and be accepted?"

"I don't think your 'Bomb Hanoi' button would fit in. They're demonstrating for peace, not more destruction."

"Peace?" I wasn't sure, but I may have been sneering. "They're so for peace that they bomb buildings and kill innocent people and then spit on soldiers while accusing them of the same thing? Hypocrisy? Jeez, let me think about that. And besides, I only wore that button once to piss off your pals at that art show you forced me to go to."

"I told you that my friends are not involved in anything that involves violence or killing," Gwen shouted. She turned and disappeared into the living room. "I don't have to defend…," she trailed off.

The conversation was routine except this time she didn't counter with the exploits of my *gangster friends*. She knew of Madge Wilson's death and wouldn't disparage her name or the sons that had buried her.

I followed through the archway and saw Gwen leaning over the glass coffee table. She stood and spun around. Her outstretched arms held a newspaper. Most people won't readily recognize a photo of themselves in a newspaper. It's not like seeing a clear, crisp reflection in a mirror, but instead is a mass of shaded dots bunched into an image. The contorted snarl on my face in the photo further slowed the recognition. But, yes, it was a picture of me. And the caption: *Gangster's pal attacks press*. Didn't I…?

"And who is this demonstrator?" Gwen asked.

"They were disrupting Mrs. Wilson's funeral. These are the bastards that support the scum who killed her." I backhanded the paper. "Don't tell me you read this trashy rag."

"My director bought this late night edition and recognized you in the picture," Gwen said, lowering the paper. "He wasn't too happy with the reputation that it would put on me if others found out. He knows the publisher and called him to ask if he would squash the picture from future editions."

"I knew there was something I didn't like about him." I felt a passing flush of embarrassment over getting Gwen in trouble with her boss, but I continued. "Typical Uncle Joe Stalin tactics. Remove any traces so it never existed."

"Don't you dare paint him with your broad brush and narrow mind," Gwen scolded as she tossed the paper onto the table. "You sound like that Senator McCarthy did, denouncing anyone who disagrees with you."

"Oh, the opposition doesn't?"

"The man was born in Russia when the czars were in power. He knows about totalitarianism and he doesn't want it happening here."

"Here? But your relatives came from Eastern Europe, too, like mine. You should be very aware of what they escaped, the bastards who took the place of the czars and who have murdered ten times more people than the czars; why our relatives scrubbed floors or shoveled shit just to be *here*, to be free from what they left."

"And this government is shoveling an unjust war down our throats and trying to take away those freedoms."

"Oh, please. Who's been brainwashing you?"

"I've had enough of this nonsense." Gwen waved her arms and started for the bedroom. "I don't have time to argue about something we're obviously never going to see eye to eye on. I have to get ready for a road tour."

"Thanks for telling me," I said as I followed.

"It just came up last night." Gwen pulled a suitcase from her side of the closet. "I'm getting a shot as temporary choreographer for a week at a trial run of our show in Poughkeepsie. They want to test the show in a small town market. It's a great opportunity."

"I'm sure. I wish you well." I felt disappointed. "I would've liked to have gone along."

Gwen spun around from the closet. "And why can't you?" Her face was consolatory. "You can meet the rest of the cast that you don't know. You'll see that they're not the ogres you think they are."

"I...I have something really important to take care of this weekend. Like I said, I would've liked to."

"Really important?" Now *she* looked disappointed. "More important than my happiness?"

"That's not fair." I spun away. "You always pull this crap. Why is your career more important than what I want to do?"

"Because you never want to do your important things with me."

"It's something you wouldn't want anything to do with." Damn, there's no way I could tell her what I was planning. But then, was anything really going to happen this weekend? Or was anything going to happen at all? "It's guy things."

"With your buddies?"

"Of course. My gangster buddies."

She smiled. "You said it, not me." She folded her arms. "OK, so you're doing your guy things and I'll be doing my girl things and we'll see each other when it's over."

I was sure she was screaming inside to tell me to be careful and not get involved in anything illegal or dangerous, but she was so damn gracious when it came to anything other than our political disagreements. "Don't worry, I'm only helping Johnny and Pete clear up some of their mother's affairs."

"They don't have an attorney?"

"It's physical stuff, like moving and driving and, you know, like that."

"They don't...?"

"Come on. They need my help and that's it!"

"Fine." She sounded rejected. "Well..." She put the last of her clothes in the suitcase and snapped the lid closed. "If you were done before Wednesday maybe you'd consider coming to Poughkeepsie. Except for Sunday. We have off and everyone is driving to a music festival at some farm about an hour or so away. I'll give you the address and directions to our hotel in Poughkeepsie."

"Sounds good. I'll definitely try to get there. You want me to drive you to the bus station or somewhere?"

"I'm driving up with Shirley and Harry. They're meeting me here."

"You sure you won't get your ear chewed off before you get to Poughkeepsie? I mean, you gotta admit that she is one obnoxious person, no matter what your point of view on politics."

"I'm going to request her silence so I can study the script, and then maybe take a nap. If she wants me to keep her newly expanded role intact, she'll be quiet."

"Rank has its privilege, huh?"

"I don't know how much rank or privilege is involved, but I'll take advantage of any I can get." Gwen scribbled the Poughkeepsie information on a large blank sheet of paper and explained the directions to me. She flipped over the paper. "This is a flyer for the event we'll be at on Sunday, just in case you're in that area," she added.

"When is your ride going to be here?" I glanced at the flyer, folded it, and placed it in my shirt pocket.

Gwen looked at her watch. "Hmm, in about fifteen minutes."

"OK, I'm gone. I don't need to see her." I put my arms around Gwen. "Can I do anything for you before I go?"

"Thanks, I'm all set." She looked up into my eyes with her baby-blues. "With my packing anyway. Quickie time, or do we anticipate a Poughkeepsie happening?"

We kissed, and again, then clung together as we sidestepped toward the bed. Then the doorbell rang, loud, jangling, like a fire alarm.

"Shit." I think we both said it.

"They're never early," Gwen sighed.

"Shirley must know I'm here and what we intended to do. Well, it'll be anticipation. That and absence makes the heart grow fonder."

"See, there's that poetry man I love, even when you use clichés." She slapped my chest as she drew away. "How can someone who once had the passion to be a writer be such a conservative?"

"What's in a name? You liberals are the ones that like to hang labels."

Brrrinnng!

"I better see you in Poughkeepsie," Gwen said with a positive tone.

"I'll try my very best." We kissed again, and then I started for the hall door. I swung it open as Gwen buzzed the ground floor entrance door lock tripper. I blew a kiss and started down the squeaking wooden stairs.

"Oh, the Fascist is here." Shirley tried to hide her words in an aside to Harry as they rounded the landing between the first and second floors—or did she?

Screw you, you fat Commie bitch. "Well, it's Mama Shirley and Papa Harry. Have a good, safe trip to Poughkeepsie," I said as my back rubbed down the tin insert wall in squeezing past the couple. "And I mean that." I turned back when I reached the landing. "Only because you're transporting my sweetie."

I continued to the ground floor, not hearing Shirley's mumbled response.

The dark, cool hallway gave way to a hot sun as I made my way through enemy turf, ignoring leftist fliers from long-haired teens and gazes from older, longer-haired, so-called revolutionaries who knew how I thought and who felt I had no right living there. My protective armor was my relationship with Gwen and her subsequent relationship with the artsy-fartsy crowd. My year-old Mustang was never molested, except for tickets. The locals knew it was mine, and they probably protected it while trying not to puke from frustration. They were probably waiting for the day that their revolution was successful and they could eliminate people like me. But then, I was just as sure that there would come a day when everything would go back to normal and all these aberrations would vanish and I would find the Mustang done in by some namesake of our old gang, the Vandals. Jeez, those were the days.

CHAPTER SIX

It was the first time that I was privileged to be invited into the inner sanctum of the back rooms of the club. But *privilege* was not necessarily the word in this case. The room was only big enough for a conference table and six chairs. The walls were paneled with a dark wood that compressed the feel of the area and, together with the light of only two wall sconces, made someone new to the setting feel like they were being constricted. Johnny and Pete sat across the glossy conference table from me. The air smelled of pine cleaner and furniture polish.

"You are one lucky son of a bitch," Johnny said. "If Lenny knew where you lived, you'd have been, at the least, in a hospital last night. Why the hell did you push him so far?"

"Hey, I'm sorry," I said. "I want to help and you guys wouldn't let me in. I saw my opportunity and I took it."

"And I asked you not to get involved," Pete said angrily. "I talked to you like I always have, like you're our brother."

"And I truly appreciate that." I flipped my hand toward Johnny. "But if I'd been a third brother, I would've been involved from the very beginning."

"No, you wouldn't. You are the other brother, who we don't involve in our business affairs, and who doesn't want to be involved," Johnny said.

"This is not business. This is retaliation for personal wrongs."

"But it also involves business, and we wouldn't be able to right the family wrongs if not for the cooperation from the business end. When Lenny couldn't find you, he went straight to Benny and Kelly. They are highly pissed and want your skull as much as Lenny does."

"Well, I figured that one wrong," I said, still not uncomfortable with the situation because of whom I was facing. "I thought he'd be too embarrassed to tell anyone I conned him."

"This is too damn important for anyone to think solely about himself," Pete said. "Not Lenny, us, or anyone else involved can do anything to jeopardize what's going down." Pete leaned back into his chair and stared at me. "So why should anyone consider involving you, who obviously are thinking only about yourself and how you can be a big hero with the ol' gang?"

"We keep going back to me thinking that I am concerned and therefore involved. I'm not trying to impress anyone. Not even you two guys. I just want to help. Period."

"So much so that you lied about me giving you the dope on the *caper*?" Pete's eyes narrowed.

"Caper? Jeez, I didn't think he'd use that word again. Look, I only said that to Lenny to get him to open up. I retracted it right off. There's no way I'd have gotten you into a jam. You know that."

Pete slouched forward and leaned on his elbows. "Yeah, I know." He looked at Johnny. "You want the floor?"

"If we let you…help us, will you knock off your shit after that?" Johnny asked me.

"You know it, man. Just tell me what…"

"It's no goddamn game, Jimmy," Johnny shouted.

The words rang in my ears and I stared into angry eyes I had never seen before. They burned into my brain and I was suddenly afraid. The pine scent was making me ill. This was not the guy I had grown up with, shared secret thoughts with, and had special memories of. This was the hard, cold businessman that had reached and maintained his position by playing with fire every day of his life.

"I'm very aware of that, John. I am serious." I had never called him simply "John." Maybe the formality struck a chord of importance.

"OK. But a warning, a very strong warning." Johnny's gaze hadn't lost its intensity. "Kelly and Benny have told Lenny that if you do one thing wrong—I mean, one tiny infraction that he sees as a threat to the operation…"

I shuddered. I knew what he was about to say, and I felt the grasp of fear. Reality was, indeed, setting in. Then I recovered and hoped they didn't see the spasm, thinking me now weak.

"And you know he will," Pete said. I had missed the end of Johnny's sentence. "We've kept you in one piece and breathing by calling in favors. You better be worth the effort in what we want you to do."

I was suddenly sitting before two employers about to give me a task. The two friends, the almost brothers, had left the room and these managers had taken their place.

"Red has a special mission to accomplish that involves some military equipment," Johnny said. "Since you are the only other guy we trust that's been in the military, we convinced Kelly to let you help Red. It's not that one of us couldn't pull it off, but when you spend four years being ordered around and living a certain way, it tends to stay with you for a long time and show in your demeanor. You'll have to get your head into it again. And you'll do everything Red tells you."

"Absolutely," I said with my hand raised as though taking an oath.

"Remember, none of your wiseass remarks. You're going to be face-to-face with military officers who will smell a rat if you act in any way disobedient. In fact, don't say a word unless spoken to."

"I understand."

"What you have to do will take only a couple of hours," Johnny said. "Once it's done, you're through. You will have nothing whatsoever to do with anything else that follows. Your obligation to everyone involved will be satisfied. You'll be off the hook with Kelly and Benny and most of all, with Lenny. We don't want to see your face around here for a full month from now. You got that?"

I wanted to protest, to push for a bigger role, but reason springs from fear and I became grateful for both my reprieve from Lenny and for being given any task at all, even though they were only tossing me a bone for my loyalty. "That last part will be hard," I said quietly. "Will you, at least, tell me what went down after the month is up?"

"Probably not." Johnny glanced at Pete, then back to me. "But we'll see. Now, I want you to get together with Red." He looked at his watch. "He should be here by now. You and Red go somewhere away from here and he'll clue you in as to what he needs you to do."

"OK." I bowed my head and then looked at them. "You guys take care of yourselves. Get the bastards but come back safe and sound." I smiled, trying to suppress the business atmosphere. "After all, you won't have me there to watch your backs."

Johnny smiled thinly, almost as though he were forcing the expression. "You take care, too. You're up first. Just remember that what you're doing will help us finish the job."

They're giving me more pep talks. Damn, this sucks. I stood and pointed at the door. "Is anyone but Red out there?"

Johnny stood and moved to the door with Pete behind him.

"Yeah. Just about everyone," Johnny said as he opened the door. He saw me hesitate. "Yes, Lenny's there. Just walk out with Red. Nothing's going to happen."

I suddenly wondered about their sincerity, these old and cherished friends who I once trusted with my life, and who I now doubted. Maybe it was because Johnny held the door for me. It was a routine we had when we were kids that after a confrontation you always let the bad guy leave the room first and he got his ass kicked by everyone waiting outside the door. Was Lenny there waiting for me? Was all this talk just bullshit to put me at ease before Lenny shoved a blade between my ribs? Was...*Ah, hell!* Get real.

I patted Pete on the shoulder and Johnny on his arm as I stepped into the hall that joined the back rooms and led to the rear of the club area. *No Lenny.* I continued to the entrance into the club and stepped into the pool hall. The fresh smell of pine faded and was replaced with the odor of beer and cigarette smoke. None of the three tables were in use. There were no bowlers in the alleys to the left. I passed the well-lit and brightly colored but quiet jukebox and turned right, through an arch and into the bar. And there they were.

Benny was behind the bar. His dark curly hair and chubby face were tinted in blue from the droplights behind him. Everyone involved in the operation occupied six of the red cushioned stools along the padded and tufted red vinyl face of the bar. It was a private party, members only. Benny had often closed the place to the public when he wanted absolute secrecy, no strangers that might intentionally listen at a back room door or overhear something they shouldn't through the thin walls of the restrooms. This was one of those nights.

They all faced Benny, sipping a drink or in quiet conversation among themselves. No one acknowledged my presence. Red finally looked my way, stood, and motioned for me to follow him. I was getting the silent treatment. Better than a beating, or worse. I moved quickly along the bare wooden floor and passed the others, trying to hold my composure, trying not to look at anyone, not even out of the corner of my eye.

I knew when I passed Lenny, feeling the cold chill of his glare that I knew was coming at me from the reflection in the mirror behind the bar. Would he try something even though he had been told not to? He *was* called "Crazy Lenny." There was a reason for that. I was so rigid I thought I'd crack right there in front of him. No, I made it past him. OK. Follow Red out the door. *Good night, all. Have fun. See you in a month. I hope.*

CHAPTER SEVEN

The cinder block façade of the recently built Long Island armory could have passed for a two-story office building, no resemblance at all to the castlelike fortresses located in New York City. It sprawled along a full block to the cyclone fence topped with barbed wire that housed the parking and storage area. The blacktop yard held a variety of camouflaged jeeps, pickups, and two-and-a-half and five-ton trucks. A one-story brick building at the far end of the property housed the motor pool.

The palms of my hands were sweaty, and I felt uncomfortable in army fatigues, particularly with three stripes and a rocker on the sleeves. Impersonating a staff sergeant: would that bring extra jail time if we were caught?

I glanced at Red behind the wheel. He had been promoted, too, displaying captain's bars on the collars of the olive drab fatigues. He had said that a little more rank would make the task easier. He had said many things the night before. He had briefed me on the plan with only what I needed to know. He had supplied the uniforms, boots, and equipment but had forgotten to have name tags made. I had been tasked to visit an army and navy store that would make up the tags immediately, while Red made some last-minute contacts and preparations. Since we were in our old neighborhood in Queens that night and I didn't feel like traveling back to Manhattan to an empty apartment, I asked my mother to sew on the name tags, telling her that the uniforms were for one of Gwen's productions. I had stayed overnight at my parents' apartment, only managing about an hour of sleep. My nerves were jangled, but I was ready for what had to be done.

It was less than an hour before sunset as we drove by the compound a second time.

"Awfully quiet in there," I said.

"Just how we want it," Red replied.

Red parked the Ford Fairlane two blocks away on a residential street. Someone would pick up the car later that night. We walked to the armory and through the unlocked steel front door unchallenged. We found the facility commander's office at the rear of the string of empty, mostly dark offices on the second floor. It was empty.

The thud of our boot heels on the tile floors was the only sound along the hall as we retraced our steps. We descended the metal stairs and found our way to the spacious cement drill floor. Steel angled beams supported the ceiling forty feet above. The room smelled of canvas tents, damp cardboard, and the soft pulpwood of crates. There were random stacks of supplies scattered over the floor.

"This is the worst goddamn National Guard unit I have ever seen," Red complained. "And that's good for our purposes, but I'd still like to have these guys for just one week. I'd straighten out their butts."

We finally saw a living, breathing person. I knew he was breathing because I could hear him snoring from across the drill floor. The soldier, lying on his back on a green wooden bench, stirred from his nap. His bench was partially hidden behind a stack of wooden boxes, and he didn't see us until we were standing at his feet.

"Are you comfortable, Private Henderson?" Red asked with authority as he read the young soldier's name tag.

Henderson rolled to his feet. "Sorry, sir. I was…" He rubbed his eyes. "I was taking a break and dozed off."

"A break from what?" Red spit out.

"I was moving some vehicles around the yard and…"

"Where is everyone?" Red was obviously annoyed. "Put on your hat, Henderson."

"It's Major Kenyon's birthday." He picked up his hat from the bench and placed it on his head. "I think the officers and NCOs took him to a civilian restaurant for dinner." He tried to smooth out his rumpled fatigues. "What can I do for…?"

"Duty hours are over?" Red looked at his watch. "They didn't leave any security personnel?"

"Yeah, I guess me. The civilian custodian who usually mans the front desk went home sick. He said they were sending a replacement, but I haven't seen any yet. And the two other enlisted permanent parties were called over to the Jamaica Armory in Queens to pick up something supposedly very important."

"And your officers still went out to dinner?"

"Oh, no, sir. This all happened after they left."

"Then why didn't you call them to come back?"

"They are coming back, sir. They have to sign out." Henderson gestured sheepishly. "And, I…I can't remember where they said they were going."

Red shook his head. "Well, I can't wait around for them. You're going to have to get me these two vehicles." He whipped a paper from his breast pocket. "Immediately."

"I…" Henderson unfolded and read the orders. "I don't think I'm authorized to…"

"You're the only one here. You are the authority. Now let's find them."

"Couldn't you wait for a few more minutes, sir? I'm not even full time. I'm just making up a couple of days for the weekend I missed. Couldn't you wait until…?"

"I've got to move these vehicles to division HQ upstate tonight." Red pointed toward the upstairs offices. "Call whoever you want, but get me those vehicles now!"

"Well, sir, I don't know who I'd call." He fumbled with the orders, seemingly reading them several times. "You say you're from division, sir?"

"That's right, private. Would you like me to call the general to have him personally OK these orders for you?"

"No. No, sir, that won't be necessary. I will need your signature, though, on the motor pool sign-out sheet."

"Let's go."

We exited the building and crossed the yard. We stopped at a line of M37 pickup-style cargo trucks, all of their beds covered with canvas tops. Henderson pointed one out to us.

"This is one," Henderson said. "Shall I check the contents for you, sir?"

"No, they're sealed in. Show the sergeant where the other vehicle is."

Henderson looked at the orders and then at the bumper numbers of the M37s. "It's this one, right next to the other."

"Good. Take the sergeant to the motor pool office and get the keys and sign-out sheets while I check the seals."

I was uneasy for a moment. I wasn't expecting to be more than a few steps from Red during the show, but dealing with this private wouldn't be difficult at all. I followed him to the motor pool building. There was a strong odor of gasoline and used oil in the spacious building.

"Sorry to say, sarge, but your captain is a real hard-ass," Henderson said as we entered the motor pool office. "He must have been regular army at one time."

"Yes, private. I think he was in Nam."

Henderson screwed up his face as he lifted two sets of ignition keys from a hook board. "That's why I'm here and not there. I don't know how you feel, but I can tell you that if our unit was ever activated, I'd be headed for Canada."

I felt my face flush. I was about to jump all over his ass—as both a sergeant and as myself—when a car horn blared from the direction of the gate.

We stepped into the yard and I saw two civilian cars enter the lot. Someone in fatigues was holding the gate open. Damn! We almost beat them out of here. *Now what?*

Henderson, still holding the ignition keys and sign-out sheets on a clipboard, veered off toward the two cars. They were parked in the darkening shadow of the main building and the passengers were climbing out.

I walked to Red, who stood between the two trucks. We watched the group of about ten soldiers gather around the gesturing Henderson.

"Red, what are we...?"

Red held up his index finger. "Stay military. Keep your cool. You're an army sergeant. Act it." He started toward the newcomers.

I straightened my posture and followed. My palms were sweaty again, and now my mouth was dry.

"Good evening, major." Red snapped to a halt and saluted. I followed suit. "And happy birthday, sir."

The middle-aged man with the gold oak leaves on his collars returned the salute. "Thank you. What can we do for you, captain?"

"I'm sure Private Henderson has explained my orders and request, sir."

"Yes, somewhat." Major Kenyon ran a finger across his thin mustache as he studied the orders given to him by Henderson. He lifted the paper higher to catch what fleeting light was available. "But why don't you tell me what the rush is?"

"Umm, sir, may I talk with you in private?" Red gestured toward the middle of the yard. "My mission is confidential."

Kenyon turned to his group. "Return to your stations, tidy up for the night, and sign out. And thank you for a wonderful dinner."

They saluted and gave a mixture of replies.

"Is your sergeant privy to your mission?" Kenyon asked as he followed Red and me to the line of trucks.

"Yes, sir. We will each drive one of the two vehicles." Red nodded. "I'm sure you know they were delivered here yesterday into your temporary care."

"Why, uh, yes. I believe the motor pool NCO took care of that transaction."

"Well, sir, we have to drive the final leg to division HQ in Albany. Something very hush-hush, which is why each leg is completed by a different set of drivers."

"What's the cargo?" Kenyon asked.

"The cargo beds are wired shut and sealed. I don't know what's in them and I'm instructed to not allow anyone, including myself, to examine the contents."

"This sounds rather unorthodox." Kenyon shook his head and stared at the orders. "Why wasn't I informed that my facility was part of this chain of custody?"

"I don't know, sir. But I thought you said you knew of the delivery of the vehicles?"

"Well, yes and no." Kenyon swiped his mustache with a forefinger. "I'm going to have to call Albany for verification. Who are you to report to with the vehicles, captain?"

"General Werner, sir." Red raised his wrist and looked at his watch. "And I'm losing valuable time. I'm to be there before midnight."

Kenyon had half-turned toward the building and now turned back. "You're reporting directly to General Werner? Or to his aide, Colonel Winston?"

"I believe the general's aide is Colonel Farmer, sir. And, yes, I report *directly* to General Werner."

Kenyon turned again. "Follow me to the office. I'm going to have to call Albany."

What the hell does this guy want? Can't he take a hint? I was nervous again. My stomach twitched.

"Just a minute, sir," Red said. "Just one more thing."

Kenyon turned his head as he walked. "Yes?"

"I *cannot* waste any more time here, and I don't want you to find any trouble over delaying me." Red paused for a response but none came. "In addition, I think that any question asked by HQ about my delay might raise my conversation with Private Henderson, the only person I found at this position when I arrived. It seems that all the responsible command were away at a birthday party, forsaking the security of a military facility."

Kenyon sputtered as he returned to face Red. "How...how dare you threaten me? There were more people than Henderson here when I left."

"But not when you retuned." Red stared defiantly into Kenyon's face. "Someone might wonder about your ability to think ahead in situations. Don't believe me, sir. Ask Henderson or go see for yourself."

Kenyon placed his hands on his hips. "OK. I think I've had about enough of your insulting comments. I'll give you the benefit of the doubt. But, just remember that this state militia is run by politics. Maybe you have General Werner to report to, but I have friends in Albany, friends that are maybe higher than General Werner. You just might find that out someday. We'll meet again, Captain…" He squinted through the dusk at Red's name tag. "Marvel. Captain Marvel, that sounds familiar." He turned to me. "And you, Sergeant…Preston."

I smiled, and Red started into a slow burn as he glared at me.

"Something funny, sergeant?" Kenyon asked. He looked like he was ready to take his frustration out on me.

"Oh, no, sir," I said. "I'm just happy to know we'll soon be on our way."

Kenyon turned toward the now-lighted motor pool and waved an OK to the transportation NCO standing in the doorway. He handed the orders back to Red. We saluted and then walked to the M37s. I saw Kenyon still standing where we had left him, watching us.

"What the hell is wrong with you?" Red said just above a whisper. "You could've blown the whole deal. Damn it, I should have taken the time to read those name tags."

"It was just something I thought would lighten the tension. Nothing happened. He was too rattled and too square to think of it as a joke. Did you want me to have our real names put on the tags?"

"You just had to get your little wisecrack in, one way or another. You…"

The motor pool NCO brought us the ignition keys. We signed our pseudonyms on the log sheets and I snickered. Red was silent.

"Thanks, sarge," the motor pool NCO said. "Hey, Sergeant Preston…of the Yukon, right? I bet you get that a lot."

"Not nearly as much as you would think."

The trucks started with no problem, and Red's M37 led the way out the open gate. The beams of my headlights swept across Major Kenyon, still watching us, and then to the rear of Red's vehicle. Within a few minutes we were on a highway headed for Queens.

CHAPTER EIGHT

Red stopped his M37 on the sidewalk cutout before the oversized garage door of a warehouse and tapped twice on the horn. The two-story building continued past the door for the full block, its faded brick wall unadorned except for an occasional dimly lit, shaded window. There were no signs, no lettering advertising a company or even an address. In contrast, the buildings on the opposite side of the street had nine or ten various businesses on divided fronts with both pedestrian and garage doors, signs illuminated by bare bulbs, and many windows. Their windows were dark. Except for our activity, the street was closed for the night.

The warehouse door jerked and then rose with a clatter. The entrance alcove was dark except for the spill of light from deeper inside the garage. Red pulled into the building. I clutched, put the floor shift into low gear, and followed him in.

As soon as the rear of my vehicle cleared the doorway, I heard the heavy door clatter downward. I suddenly felt safe, not exposed to gawking drivers on the highways and streets, having to return waves to backseat children, or feeling terror when a state trooper or city police car passed us by. Military vehicles were a common site in the area and weren't scrutinized by law enforcement, but you never know when something can go wrong, like an accident or mechanical troubles that would draw the cops.

We made a ninety-degree turn toward the light and descended a concrete ramp. I saw a long silver cargo trailer parked along the outside wall. The back doors were open, and two heavy steel ramps extended from the rear sill to the ground. The trailer and ramp took up half the length of the wall, and the Peterbilt tractor with extended cab attached to the front took up a good part of the rest.

I didn't see anyone around the tractor-trailer—or anywhere in the garage. I looked in the side view mirror and saw that the door we had entered through had completely closed and that whoever had operated the control switch had also disappeared into another part of the warehouse.

Red's M37 parked directly behind the trailer, its wheels aligned perfectly with the ramps. I pulled behind Red and turned off the ignition just as he exited his truck. I could see a small cache of boxes and crates stacked against the front wall of the trailer.

"You just earned another discharge, pal," Red said as I jumped from the running board.

"I'd rather reenlist, but I guess I've had my excitement for the day."

"To tell you the truth," Red said in almost a whisper, "even with your little sideshow act, I would like to have you along, but…" He looked up and over my shoulder.

I turned and saw shadowy figures at the partially lit window of a second-story office overhang against the inside wall. It was the rest of the crew waiting for my exit so they could start the next phase. They were probably chomping at the bit to get under way. I felt used up. My hour of glory was over.

"Your civvies are hanging in that john over there." Red pointed to a row of doors under the office overhang, almost hidden by two sedans—a new red and white Chevy with a dent in the right fender and a year-old black Buick—parked in front of them. One door was labeled "Men's Room." A corner staircase led to the upstairs office.

"They want you to get dressed and leave by the door on the other side of the john. You'll find a hallway that leads to an exit door that will lock behind you. There are five twenty-dollar bills in the pocket of your jacket. You can catch a cab on Queens Boulevard, a couple blocks north of here."

"That's it, huh?" I looked at my boots. "I even get a paycheck."

"Stop stalling, Jimmy. We have to get rolling soon to keep with our schedule. I'll see you again someday."

"Good luck, Red. It was a pleasure working with you, and…" We shook hands. "Shazam, Captain Marvel."

Red smiled. "Get out'a here, Preston."

I didn't look up at the office windows as I walked to the men's room. The white tiled interior had a strong, sweet odor of urine cakes. I saw my clothes on hangers clipped on one of the gray metal stall doors and my sneakers on the floor under them. I quickly stripped off the uniform, folded it, and placed it on one of the sinks and the boots underneath. I had already removed the web belt for ease of driving and had left it under the driver's seat of the M37. I dressed in the blue T-shirt, dungarees, and jacket I had been wearing in the morning.

Just as I started toward the rear exit, the front door squeaked open. I turned around. Lenny slammed the door closed behind him and glared at me. His pointy face glistened with sweat.

"You say a word and I'll put a fuckin' bullet in your head," he growled. His hand reached inside the opening of his cracked brown leather jacket. "I got something to get off my chest and I'll make it quick. You fucked me up with Benny and Kelly and I'm one step from their shit list. I don't care if you're under Johnny's wing." His arm dropped to his side. "When I get back, you're gonna pay for what you did."

"Lenny, I can't tell you how much I'm sorry about…"

"Shut the fuck up, I said." His hand reached the jacket zipper and then dropped back to his side again. "You better take that one month they gave you and find another city to live in 'cause if you're anywhere near this one, your ass is mine. You won't be able to hide in anyone's shadow."

There was no arguing with him. I tried to act even more humble. "OK, but I really mean it, that I'd do anything to make up for…"

"Get the fuck out'a here." Lenny pointed to the back door. "If we find you in this building or see your face after two minutes, you're dead!"

I held up my hands in surrender. "I'm gone." I turned and then wondered if I should have my back to him. I walked stiffly to the rear door, opened it, and heard a squeak. I turned slightly as I stepped into the rear hall. The front door had just closed. Lenny was gone.

I was sure his threat was strictly his idea. Benny and Kelly had no reason to intimidate me any further. They knew I did as I was told. Well, most times.

And the way Lenny moved his hand away from the gun—if, in fact, there was a gun—when he mentioned Johnny's name led me to believe that he respected Johnny's position. Lenny had probably snuck away from his duties for a moment to let me know I was still on the hook with him. It didn't matter how well I had performed my part. This was personal.

In the dozen or so years I had known Lenny, he had never swallowed an insult nor had a con pulled on him. He had to have retribution. He remained very dangerous and scary.

But that was surely only one of the risks I faced when I went along on the rest of the operation. *Yes, I was going.* How, I didn't know, but I had a feeling they needed me. And if I proved myself—both to myself first and then to them— maybe all this crap that had gotten out of hand would end and the status quo would return. But who knows? *I would just have to see.*

I was standing there holding the rear door open, staring at the front door, and half expecting it to fly open with Lenny shouting, "Time's up." I had no plan and time *was* about up.

I looked up and down the rear hall. The exit sign over the door at the far end of the hall gave the space a red glow. Two doors at even intervals were along the men's room wall. The street wall was empty. There was a staircase at the opposite end of the hall, and I was sure it was a second access to the upstairs office. There could be someone at the top of the stairs listening for the exit door to close.

I stopped at the first door and put my ear to the surface. No sounds. I tried the knob. Locked. I continued to the exit door and leaned on the crash bar. The door opened onto the street. I let it swing completely open so it would close slowly. I stepped back and tried the knob of the second door. It turned freely and I was in the room. The exit door slammed loudly as I closed the hall door and snapped the button lock closed.

The room was semi-dark, with light from the garage filtering through Venetian blinds on a picture window. I swerved around a stack of wooden crates in the middle of the floor and made my way to the window. I peeked between the slats and found I was in the room just past the Chevy. There was a buzz of activity around the trailer. I glanced at the door that opened into the garage and saw that it was bolt-locked. *OK. I was safe for the moment.*

I watched for fifteen minutes while I tried desperately to formulate some kind of plan. Nothing seemed plausible, except maybe to steal one of the cars. Would they be using both? Maybe one would be left behind and I could use it to follow them. *No.* Why would they both be here if not to be used? I had to wait for some opportunity.

Red had moved one of the M37s slowly and cautiously up the ramps, and now the truck that I had driven followed. Pete was driving it and was having trouble working the clutch. He had made it halfway, with the engine racing and then slowing down as he tried to coordinate his clutch and gas. He slipped back a few feet each time the tires lost traction.

"Careful, Pete," Johnny shouted from beside the ramps. "We don't want this cargo spilling into our laps."

Sonny Krause, in his form-fit white T-shirt showing off his muscular torso, stood next to the two Looney brothers and behind Johnny. The three watched and swayed with body language and hand gestures to support Pete's efforts.

Sonny was a head shorter than the Looneys, who were both six foot two and more brawny than a sculptured muscular like Sonny. Pat and Mike Looney's real name had been Clooney, but it was changed by everyone in the old crowd to reflect their reckless nature. Their identical features of size, blond straw–textured, medium-length hair hanging over their ears, strong jawline, and rosy faces made them appear to be twins, but they had been born a year apart. They wore identical green shamrock-emblazoned polo shirts and dungarees, further projecting the twin image.

The brake light went off and Pete's M37 rolled backward before the engine roared and propelled the vehicle onto the trailer floor beyond the ramps.

Sonny and the Looney brothers cheered and clapped from behind Johnny. Pete appeared at the trailer opening and bowed. Arms outstretched, he staged a circus aerialist balancing act down one of the ramps.

I wished I were out there with them. I wished I were enjoying the light moments along with the drudgery. I felt left out and started to sink into a funk. *Snap out of it, you jerk!* Stay focused. You'll be with them eventually.

Red appeared at the trailer opening carrying a pair of bolt cutters. He announced that everything was ready and jumped to the garage floor. They all pitched in to work the ramps into their sectioned retractable position and slide the assemblies into a compartment under the trailer. The trailer doors were slammed shut with a bang. Pete began to slide the locking hasp into place and then stopped.

"Where the hell's the lock?" Pete asked. He opened one of the doors and looked inside. "Not here."

Johnny shrugged, and the others looked over their shoulders or on the ground.

"I thought you had it," Johnny said.

"No, I...I think it may be in one of the rooms where we took the boxes from."

"Well, let's find the damn thing," Johnny said as he looked at his watch. "We only have ten minutes before we pull out."

Pete cupped his hands around his mouth and shouted at the overhead office. "Lenny. Look and see if the trailer lock is up there."

The six on the garage floor scattered and I saw Sonny coming toward me. I ducked back from the blinds. The doorknob rattled. Then Sonny passed the window and the knob of the next door rattled. "These are locked," Sonny yelled. Then I heard the men's room door squeak.

I looked out both sides of the blinds and was able to see the entire area. The garage floor was empty of people. The others were probably checking the rooms on the cross street side of the building. *Should I?*

The rear door of the men's room opened and I heard Lenny shout inside, "What's wrong with you guys? I'm on the phone with Benny telling him everything is going along on schedule and all of a sudden everything stops because you can't find a fuckin' lock?"

"Take it easy, man," Sonny replied. "We'll find it."

The urinal flushed and I heard them both in the rear hall.

"Check these rooms," Lenny said.

"I already did from the garage. They're locked."

"No. Check them from this side. I think I left one open. And make sure that exit door is locked. I wouldn't put it past that Jimmy character to have wedged it so it could be opened from outside. I'll look upstairs again."

Oh, oh. Now. I have to do it now before Sonny finds a door locked that should be open or Lenny looks out that office window. I could hear his footfalls on the steps. Slowly. *Take your time.* I quietly slid the bolt open as the knob on the rear door rattled. I slipped into the garage and gently closed the door behind me. *What if…Shut up!*

I looked both ways like a kid crossing a street. *No one.* I felt my heart pound and my feet dart forward. I sprinted hard toward the trailer. *Don't look back. Don't look up. He's not there yet. He's not up the stairs yet.* One of the trailer doors was angled open, and I took a running leap through the gap, landed short, and smacked my thighs against the rear body sill. Right at impact I had twisted my body and pushed against the closed door. I continued forward and landed inside with a soft thud. I had fallen on top of a bunch of quilted moving mats. I didn't move. I sucked in musty-smelling air coming off the mats and hoped the pounding of my heart didn't drown out voices or noises from the garage that I needed to hear. *Calm down. I think I made it. No. Not entirely, yet.*

From what I could sense, there had been no movement or sounds in the minute I lay frozen on the floor. They would be back here soon. I stood and surprisingly felt no pain in my thighs. I was glad I still kept my leg muscles in shape by walking whenever possible.

The only place to hide was inside one of the M37s. The closest was about five feet from the rear doors. There were chains stretched from six points on the vehicles to rings in the steel floor. Wooden chocks were behind each tire. The canvas was no longer secured with cable. Red had broken the security seal, probably to inspect and inventory the cargo. The top was buttoned to the rear gate with clips and tabs. I unloosened most of them and slid between the canvas and gate. There were what appeared to be a group of three-foot-high oxygen tanks taking all but enough space for me.

"Here it is," I heard someone shout from somewhere outside and in front of the trailer.

I lifted the canvas, out of curiosity, before the trailer doors were closed and the light disappeared. Oxygen tanks? No, they were yellow in color and smaller and thinner than oxygen cylinders. And the fittings on the tops were different. They were lined five abreast with more rows behind them, secured with heavy chains.

"It was in the cab," Pete said, almost at the back doors.

I lifted the canvas a tad higher to read the almost faded lettering and saw SARIN (GB). I dropped the canvas. *My God. Sarin.* Seconds later the rear door slammed shut. I was being sealed in with a massive quantity of one of the deadliest chemical killers known to man. The hasp snapped shut and the lock clicked—or was entombed more appropriate? What the hell were these guys going to do with this stuff? My guys. My pals. What were they planning to do with this deadly crap?

I had learned about sarin along with an array of other chemical weapons during NBC—nuclear, biological and chemical training while in the air force. It only had one use, and that was to kill people. Were Johnny and Pete going to unleash this shit on the people who killed their mother?

The diesel engine of the tractor roared to life. The signature loud rattling, like a powerful coffee grinder, reverberated through the garage.

I was beginning to feel uncomfortable with my back pressed against the cylinders, not physically, but mentally. I wondered if there might be a leak in one of them that would be masked by the smell of the canvas. No, sarin was odorless. But there still could be a leak that would make me go into spasms with drooling and choking and...I lifted the canvas to flee. *Get hold of yourself.* If there was a leak, it would get you anywhere in this trailer. If you move around, you're going to make noise and they'll find you out. But maybe *now* I didn't want to go. Let them find me and get me the hell out of here.

It's too late. You're locked in. You're committed and packaged. Ready to go. Several sounds penetrated the thin aluminum walls. An overhead motor lifted open the cross street door. Automobile engines started. People were shouting last-minute acknowledgments and directions. Then it was all suddenly overwhelmed by the Detroit diesel as it was coaxed into gear and tugged its load into the street. Yeah, it was too late. You wanted this, and what is it they say about wishing for something?

I waited until the eighteen-wheeler was off side streets and on a continuous run along what seemed to be a highway before I climbed out of the M37. I had put the irrational fear of a sarin leak out of my mind. In the closeness and darkness of the trailer, I had no other choice but to still trust I was doing the right thing. I convinced myself that whatever they were going to do was also the right thing. *I'm here and I'm staying.*

Within twenty minutes we were crossing a bridge. We stopped for most likely a tollbooth and then continued along more highways.

I was beginning to relax. Anxiety had kept me awake the night before, and I wasn't going to keep that stress bottled up for another night. It had been a grueling day. I stumble-stepped into the open space behind the M37, trying to recall where the outstretched chains were and not trip on them. I crouched to gather the padded mats and folded them into a fairly thick mattress. As I bedded down, I had a feeling this was going to be a long journey. I had to get some shut-eye before the next phase unfolded. The rocking of the trailer, even the clinking of the deadly sarin cylinders, overcame the musty odor alongside my face and I fell asleep.

CHAPTER NINE

I awoke in the same darkness and stale air. The musty smell of my mattress hit my nostrils first, followed by the odor of the canvas covers of the M37s. It reminded me of a night in a hot tent. I listened for a moment and heard nothing but the hum of tires, an occasional clinking of the cylinders, and the constant rattle of the stowed M37s. I coughed. My throat was dry and my lungs labored to catch a full breath.

My knees cracked as I stood and stretched the aches from my muscles. Pains shot through my thighs for an instant. I kicked the padded mats to the sidewall so I wouldn't trip over them in the dark. The trailer drifted into a turn and I followed the mats into the aluminum side panel, bounced off the resilient material, and did a dance to keep my balance. In the total darkness, I felt like I was being jerked around some amusement park funhouse.

Wait a minute. I remembered the web belt I had worn with the fatigues. I staggered along a clear strip next to the far wall to avoid tripping on the taut chains, and then reached the cab of the M37. I fumbled under the front seat and found the belt. I shook the canteen. Empty. I removed the right angle shaped flashlight and clicked it on. It worked.

I returned to the rear of the trailer and shone the beam in a slow arc across the doors. There were vents along the tops. I stepped to the doors and pulled on the handle of a rod that ran alongside the hinge post joint. The louvers creaked open, and I felt a downdraft of sweet country air. I tugged the handle on the other door, and it was like turning on an air conditioner.

I took a few deep breaths and coughed several times before my lungs adjusted to the change in atmosphere. My throat was still dry, and I wished I had filled the canteen instead of opting for less weight hanging on my hips.

I aimed the flashlight beam at my wristwatch. Five o'clock. Five AM. I had slept for about four hours. I was sure the caravan hadn't stopped, as the sudden change in motion would've wakened me. They would have to stop soon to change drivers or gas up. By the feel of the ride, we were still on a highway or some other smooth pavement. We continued along the same uneventful stretch of road for another half an hour.

With a jolting ripple under the floor, the terrain changed. I was hurled into the rear of the M37. I heard the air brakes hiss and I was pressed against the tailgate. The brakes released, and I tumbled backward onto the floor. The ride became an undulating earthquake. The air brakes hissed again, and I rolled forward before calm set in.

I heard voices and turned off the flashlight. Only the moonlight filtering through the open vents illuminated the interior. I quickly, and as softly as I could, climbed to my feet and felt my way to the forward M37. I avoided the first vehicle because I guess I was a little spooky about keeping the sarin company again. *Oh shit!* What about the opened vents? Would someone notice?

I squeezed between the lip of the tailgate and unsecured canvas top and scrunched into the crowded bed. The canvas fell back into place just as one of the rear doors of the trailer clanged open.

"They look OK." Shit, it was Lenny's voice. I sucked in a breath of canvas-flavored air.

"Check them to be sure." It was Sonny. "After we top off the tank from the spare diesel can, I gotta get behind the wheel for the last leg of the trip."

I heard scrambling, mumbling, and then footsteps alongside my M37. I held my breath again. I could feel Lenny's menacing presence. The bed shook and the chains rattled as Lenny tested the vehicle's moorings. I tried desperately to hold my breath a little longer.

My lungs felt tight and began to use up my remaining oxygen. The carbon dioxide buildup made me light-headed, and my eyes felt like they were about to explode.

Lenny moved to the rear M37 and slammed the cab door shut that I must have left ajar. I pushed my head inside my jacket to act as a sound muffler and relieved my lungs. The hot air felt like a summer breeze against my chest. I took another quick breath, most of it my exhaled carbon dioxide.

"They're both still tied down OK," Lenny said. "I'm glad Sonny's gonna be driving. I'm beat and there's no way I would find my way through these woods."

The soles of Lenny's shoes slapped the ground. "I guess you guys are going by the easy route from here?"

"Yeah." It was Red. "The other car will stick with you for a while."

The trailer door slammed shut and locked. I exhaled as I lifted my head from inside my jacket and swallowed gulps of fresh air.

I didn't hear any more conversation. It was about ten minutes until I heard the tractor engine rev to life. I waited for movement before climbing out of my hideaway. I had been so intent on keeping out of Lenny's grasp that I had forgotten to look at what was stored in this other cargo area. Thank God, it wasn't another load of sarin. Just crates. *Wait.* I shone the flashlight on the wood slats. *AR15s.* Army assault rifles, but obsolete now that the M16 was in service. These must have been snatched from some surplus warehouse. Three stacks high and two wide. What were they going to do with them? There were crates of ammo behind them, I was sure. I didn't want to disturb the setting of the boxes to investigate and could only guess. One thing was for sure, there was a really big show coming up, and I wondered for a moment whether I really wanted to be a part of it. The moment passed.

We were still on a rough, unpaved road and bumped and swayed along the route for another hour or so. There was only an occasional flash of light through the vents, leading me to believe we were traveling through a dense wooded area. I wondered if the Chevy or Buick, whichever had stayed with us, could transverse this kind of terrain.

I held the side of the M37 tightly as we started uphill and I heard the engine being powered by the low gears. It strained as the incline increased and the road surface softened. *Whack! Whack! Whack!* It sounded like a hailstorm as pebbles and rocks were thrown past the mudguards and slammed into the underside of the rear floor. No way would the Chevy or Buick make it through this passage.

The Detroit began to whine and I thought it would throw a rod, when suddenly the engine relaxed and within seconds I felt the trailer level off. We had reached a summit. The engine continued to run in low gear until we picked up momentum, then shifted to a normal drive gear.

The road was still unpaved, but nothing like the rugged slope we had just climbed. We bounced along for several miles. I looked at my watch. Two minutes to seven. I looked at the vents. The sun had replaced moonlight; the flecks of occasional sunlight were broken by fleeting shadows like flocks of birds trying to keep pace with the trailer. We were still in the woods. *Over the river and through the woods to grand…Whump!* I was thrown into the air and somehow landed back on my feet. I moved to the tailgate and clung to it. We hit two more ruts and then started into a turn.

The air brakes hissed and we rolled to a stop. We backed, went forward, backed again, and then pulled forward to straighten out. Branches crackled against both sides of the aluminum trailer. The road had narrowed. We picked up speed. Larger branches and what sounded like small trees and saplings smashed into the trailer sides. I switched on the flashlight and saw the aluminum sheeting begin to buckle inward. The material looked like tinfoil being punched by someone hanging off the roof.

An aluminum support rib bent, and the two weakened panels attached to it began to twist. Twigs rammed through the opening and sucked the bough of a four-inch tree branch into the interior like it was being stuffed into a shredder. I was pelted with chunks and splinters of soft, fresh wood. The bough widened the separation, and the panel ripped loose from the supports and from the floor. It flapped outside the trailer, and the wind rushed through the gaping hole to toss the debris of the branches into a cyclone throughout the rear of the trailer.

The panel tore completely from the floor and bent back in a triangle against the next panel like a silvery sheet folded on a prepared bed. *Why the hell don't they slow down?* I almost shouted to remind them of the cargo they were transporting.

Sonny or whoever was driving must have read my mind. We slowed and suddenly the pummeling subsided. I wobbled to the rear of the trailer and peered out the three-foot-wide opening. There were still trees whizzing by, but at a distance. I held on to the next undamaged support rib and leaned out a few inches. The entire side was damaged, including the tractor. The side view mirror was missing, its support twisted, and the fiberglass nose panel had a large elongated hole along the fender line. Boy, they did some job on this rig.

We began to slow in stages, and I let the wind, which had subsided, blow into my face. It felt great. I could see the trees in more detail. There were oaks, maples, and pine set back about ten feet, separated from the road by a strip of wild grass and weeds. We were definitely several hundred miles north of the city, but I couldn't even guess in what state.

The driver shifted into low gear again, and I saw that we were approaching a clearing about a quarter mile ahead. I sensed that we were close to our final destination, and, if I were to remain invisible, I would have to make my exit now.

They couldn't see me from the cab, but what if one of the cars had kept up with us? *No. No way.* Get ready. The clearing was coming up fast. I had to jump before the clearing so I could make it into the woods to hide when they stopped.

What if they didn't stop? *Go!* I pushed the loose panel out and leaped into space. I cleared the box and wildly rotated my arms for balance. I landed on my feet for a split second and then shot forward as my back muscles tightened. I went into a somersault, leaving a swathe through the weeds. I came to a halt on my stomach after three rolls and stayed motionless.

I waited until the tractor-trailer entered the clearing about fifty feet away before raising my head to see over the tops of the weeds. They scratched against my face and were very dry and smelled like straw. No car bringing up the rear. OK, Sonny, you can stop now. Hit those brakes, Sonny. The tires began to kick up a cloud of dust as the rig picked up speed and I realized I had jumped ship too soon. That speaks a lot for my sixth sense.

I stood and immediately collapsed as pains shot through my legs. Slowly. Get up slowly. I pushed myself to my feet again and watched as the cloud of dust rolled across a meadow of burned-out scrub grass. I limped to the road and surveyed the terrain. It was several meadows, a flat, once-grassy plain stretching for a couple of miles across to another tree line and to either side for several miles. There were mountains in the distance.

Damn! I hoped they would stop. It would be some walk to catch up, especially in the growing heat. I thought it was supposed to be cooler up north. Boy, did I screw up royally. I better start walking while I have the strength. I found a strong tree branch that had probably wedged under the trailer and separated at the same time as I did. I broke away some twigs and used the staff as a walking stick to pull me along. The back of the trailer had become a silver dot in a gray dust cloud. I was sure that the rest of my trek wouldn't be easy.

CHAPTER TEN

By the position of the sun, I figured it to be past noon. I usually didn't eat much for breakfast, so that was no loss, but now lunchtime was slipping by and my stomach growled. It was blazing hot and there was no shade on the plains of straw. I had draped my jacket over my head as a sunshade and held it horizontal with one outstretched arm, but even alternating arms with the walking stick became tiresome. The black jacket only absorbed the sun rays and the heat rather than reflect them, so I gave up the idea.

The cloud of dust that represented the trailer had made a turn and begun traveling along the length of the plain, keeping parallel with the far tree line. *With a cloud of dust and a hearty hi-ho…*God, the heat was getting to my brain. I had tried to follow, but I lost sight of the swirl after it disappeared when the tree line bent out of view. By then I was over halfway across the dried grassland. It was the point of no return.

My lips were dry. I tried to lick them, but I had no saliva in my parched mouth. I had changed course when I knew I couldn't keep up with the trailer and took about an hour to reach the second tree line. I collapsed on my back in the shade of an oak tree. My head was pounding and I found I had stopped sweating. My skin felt tight and dry. *No good.* You could get heat stroke. I needed water. Damn it, why didn't I fill that canteen? I closed my eyes and was at least thankful for being out of the sun. Leaves floated down and brushed past my face.

What's that? It couldn't be. I was sure it was nothing but my brain still frying. Is there such a thing as an audio mirage? No. I was sure that it was a proverbial babbling brook. *Come on! Don't mess around with my head.* I opened my eyes and stared at the treetops as though they would help me judge where the sound was coming from. Behind. I rolled on my stomach and pushed off the ground with my elbows before my legs would join in the effort. The walking stick helped me heave myself up onto my feet.

I limped through a stand of pines. The smell of the trees and the water seemed to cool me internally. There it was, about three feet wide, gurgling and splashing over smooth, round stones, just down a slight embankment. In my haste I stumbled, the walking stick collapsed, and I rolled down the bank to the water. My face submerged and the cold shocked me. *Easy. Take it easy. Sip.* I cupped my hands and drank and wet my face and head and neck. It was heaven. I wouldn't trade it for a case of ice-cold beer…Well, we'll see how that plays out later.

After I was done refreshing my body, my mind seemed to function more effectively. I had no vessel to carry the water, so the next best thing was to stay close to the source. Not only would I have a constant supply, but also the brook would lead me to some sort of civilization.

The trailer had to be at its destination by now. I had to find Johnny and Pete and the others if I was to help. Who knows how long before the show was to begin? I was still hungry and weak, but at least I was able to walk—barely, but able—and that's what I needed to do. The heat was still messing with my brain, and I imagined that my feet were beginning to grow roots and I would become part of the forest. I swung my jacket over my shoulder and leaned into the walking stick.

The brook wound deeper into the woods, sometimes reduced to a forced trickle or hidden underground, but it still flowed from somewhere ahead. I crunched through occasional blankets of premature dead, brown leaves and pine needles. Although the sun didn't have much of an effect on the inner canopy of the forest, it seemed to be baking some of the higher branches. A tall outcrop of rocks sometimes blocked my route, and I would have to cross on fallen trees from one bank to the other or exert my already depleted energy in climbing over or around the obstructions.

I didn't know if it was a couple of miles or more, but out of nowhere a clearing popped into view and the brook, now a wider stream, flowed into a fertile green pasture.

I reached the edge of the trees and saw people tending crops along the stream. There were small irrigation channels dug out from the stream that ran through the acres and acres of vegetation. My heart skipped like the first time I had seen Gwen. I felt love for these farmers. They were going to save my life. I guess my mind wasn't back to functioning power, but my emotions carried me along.

I tied my jacket arms around my waist, then stumbled and poked with the walking stick toward a break in rows of tall stalks of corn. They looked like a security wall surrounding the other vegetables. I could smell the difference in the richer, darker soil of the farm. Tomatoes, squash, cucumbers…Damn, this jagged leafy stuff coming up looks like…Yeah, it is. They're cannabis plants. Marijuana. That's what the wall was hiding.

I was about thirty feet away when they saw me—and when I realized they weren't ordinary farmers. They were hippies. They were long-haired hippies and their women. Hippettes? Damn, who cared about their hair? I needed their help.

"Hello, friend," the closest man said. He was in his early twenties and he wore a wide-brimmed white straw hat. He stopped working to lean on his rake. "Are you lost?"

"Yes," I said.

Three more young men in bibbed denims and three women in ankle-length dresses gathered to scrutinize me. More workers toiled on in nearby sections but ignored my entrance.

"Welcome to Nirvana," the straw-hat man said.

"Nirvana, New York?" I asked.

Straw-Hat smiled. "We have no political borders here. We only respect the individuality of human beings."

Well, how can you argue with that? These people don't seem to be kin to the New York City branch of hippies.

"Are you Amish?" I asked.

"Oh, no. Only in our belief of peace and self-reliance." Straw-Hat smiled and pointed at the marijuana crop. "I don't think they indulge in our type of recreation."

"Or practice free love," the female closest to Straw-Hat said. Strands of raven hair spilled from under her blue kerchief, and she wore the apparent uniform of the day: a gray ankle-length dress and sandals that looked like they were made out of an old tire. She was a little older than the rest, maybe mid-twenties. She smiled, and her small, unadorned face radiated. I thought of Gwen again. I smiled back and my lips cracked. I winced.

"You must have wandered off the trail," Straw-Hat said. "Don't worry, Canada isn't far."

Canada?

"You seem a bit older than the rest, but you are a draft resister, right?"

"Why, uh, yes." I felt a surge of anger pass through me for admitting—even as a lie—to that. But I needed their help. Thankfully, I looked five years younger—

as I had often been told—than my age of thirty. I remembered the hippie mantra to never trust anyone over thirty. "I had a student deferment for a while, but now they came looking for me." I scanned over the crops like reading a menu. "I could use something to eat."

"We would gladly give you something from our land, but it's all accounted for and needed for our community. You can get food at the *general store*." He emphasized the location with a wink. "It isn't far."

"General store?" Jeez, they couldn't even spare a tomato or a couple of string beans? Anything?

"Yes." Straw-Hat hesitated and eyed me suspiciously. "You do know it's the last stop on the Underground Railroad before Canada?"

I put the back of my hand to my brow and wiped the sweat. "To tell you the truth, the heat and hunger have disoriented me. I'm not thinking straight."

"Of course." Straw-Hat wiped his brow as well. "This has been an unusually hot summer for this area." He gestured upstream. "Please follow Martha back to the freedom trail."

Martha, the girl who had smiled at me, stepped forward and beckoned to me. I followed, thanking Straw-Hat and his colleagues—for what I wasn't sure—as I passed them. Martha walked briskly along a path that meandered through the crops. She held the sides of her gray dress and lifted it to her knees. I wondered if it was for freedom of movement or to show me her shapely legs.

I caught up with her just as we passed around a wall of cornstalks and out of sight of the others. She pulled a dark red apple from a pocket of her dress. "Here, this should help until you reach the general store. I believe you really are a draft resister."

I took the apple and gnawed a large chunk from it. It was crunchy and oh, so sweet, and I took another bite. "Thanks a lot," I finally said between gnashes, feeling embarrassed at my manners. "Why did you say you believe I *am* a draft resister?"

"Rather than one of them."

"Who?"

"The Renaissance."

"What's that?"

"You'll find out at the general store. Just don't join up with them. They're bad news, and you seem like a good person. I'll be done with my chores by eight o'clock, around dark."

"Yes?" I bit a final chunk of apple.

"I'd like to get the chance to convince you to stay on your course to Canada. I'd be happy to keep company with someone such as yourself."

"Such as myself?" I tossed the apple core over the tops of the cornstalks.

"A hero. All draft resisters are heroes."

I tried to keep my cool as I remembered the mayor of New York City saying that the real heroes of the war were those who went to Canada. I felt anger over a statement that had now become a rally cry for the left wing. But I had to maintain the cover they had unwittingly provided for me and forced myself to ignore my ire. I continued to follow the dark-haired naïve girl as I switched my thoughts to her proposition.

"Do you have someone you're going to meet in Canada or someone you'll return to someday?" she asked.

"Yes." Gwen's face again flashed into my mind. She *would* be waiting for me in Poughkeepsie when all this was over.

"Well, hero, they say if you can't be with the one you love, then love the one you're with."

"First off, I'm not a hero. Stop calling me a hero because I'm running away from a responsibility."

"Response…Oh, my. I see you're still struggling with a conscience. Believe me, you *are* doing the right thing."

We reached the outer wall of the cornstalk fence. The stream was now about twenty yards to our right and flowed under a small pedestrian bridge. A dirt path ran off either side of the span.

"Go left." She pointed to yet more trees about fifty yards down the path. "Just beyond the trees is a ridge that overlooks the valley and our town of Nirvana. The general store is the first building this side of town. And, please, go directly there and check in. Stay in town. Don't wander across the river." She touched my cheek. "You seem to be full of anger and doubt. You weren't meant to fight. Don't join the Renaissance. Go to Canada."

Jeez, another one who thinks I'm a cream puff.

"I have to return to my chores," she said as we stopped on the path. "Remember, eight o'clock. Please wait for me. I'd like to get to know you."

"Well, I'm going to have to rest a while. Maybe I will see you."

"You will." She turned and headed back toward the cornstalks.

"Hey…Martha. You wouldn't happen to have another apple, would you?"

She stopped and turned back. "No, I'm sorry. That was supposed to be my afternoon snack, but you needed it more. There will be plenty of food at the general store."

Damn, it was hard to hate these people. "Thank you very much. See you later."

"I hope so." She turned again and disappeared into the corn.

I suddenly applied my thoughts about Gwen to Martha, although I didn't know her well enough to have any emotional attachment. But then, I had some strange urge to protect her from this choice of lifestyle. Protect her from what? She wants to be here. Protect her from this Renaissance group? Damn, I don't know. I've got to get some food and, most important, not forget why I'm really here. I had to find the guys.

I continued my journey and passed through the wall of trees. I found the ridge just beyond and started down a gentle slope toward the valley below.

A river divided the commercial and residential town of small, mostly one-story wooden buildings from an apparently industrial section of several brick buildings towered over by three tapered, cement smokestacks. Several of the wooden buildings had peace signs and single words of peace or love painted in bright colors. A one-lane steel girder bridge about fifty feet long connected the two sections.

What immediately drew my attention was the mountain that towered behind the factory complex. The side of the mound facing me was completely denuded of any foliage. It stood like a giant barren anthill in the midst of flowering lush plant life around its base. It was an obscene boil on the green pastures of the valley. There were other, taller peaks in the distance that formed the boundaries of the valley and that were apparently unaffected. No smoke rose from the chimneys, and I was sure that they hadn't spouted whatever it was that killed that mountain for a long time.

CHAPTER ELEVEN

The path sliced down through heavy brush and ended at a dirt road that appeared to be the town's main street. The street continued through two small intersections and across the bridge as cracked and gouged asphalt before it became dirt again near the factories, then disappeared around the rear of the bald mountain.

As Martha had said, the general store was the first building I would reach. It was a sprawling one-story structure with a raised wooden sidewalk. It took up over half the frontage before the next intersection. It, like most of the buildings, seemed to have been plucked from some old west town in Arizona or Kansas. The only thing missing were horses tied up to a hitching rail out front instead of a dented, dull red, four-wheel drive Ford pickup truck parked parallel to the sidewalk. And people. The streets of the entire town were empty. The streets were quiet, but I heard a distant hum like large machinery and the sound of motorcycles revving their engines. Was that a gunshot? Two. Three. No, probably backfire. It came from across the river.

My legs ached to climb the two steps to the boardwalk. I limped up, threw away the walking stick, and straightened up, then thumped erratically along the gray wooden slats to the front doorway. The double doors were open and hooked to the wall, allowing a refreshing flow of cool air from inside. I stepped in and looked up. There were three ceiling fans evenly spaced above the store-length oak counter. Two belts drove them from an axis hub above the center fan. It was like stepping back into the past. Barrels and crates of fresh produce lined the floor in front of the counter. A sign on the wall behind the center fan read: COOPERATIVE

FARM AND COMMUNE STORE. I guess this was their terminology for general store.

There were five customers assembled around an inactive six-foot potbelly stove on the left side of the store. They were dressed in dungarees and either denim or leather vests. I thought I was back on the streets of New York City. These guys looked like one of the motorcycle gangs that broke up hippie marches or groups of the antiwar protesters who trashed military recruitment offices or ROTC buildings. Whatever their politics, they usually generated trouble. Two of them stared at me. I tried not to eyeball them and swept my gaze around the rest of the store interior.

An old red and white Coke ice chest stood in a corner under bumped-out plate glass windows. The bay windows wrapped around the front of the store and about four feet on the sides, giving a panoramic view of the entire street.

"Can I help you?" I hadn't seen the store clerk when I entered. He seemed to have materialized behind the counter in front of me. He had serious blue eyes that stared from behind granny glasses. His blond hair was tied in a ponytail.

"Where are the rest of the townspeople?" I asked as I stepped into a space at the counter between the stacked bushels.

"Working in the fields. Only a few of us have duties to perform here. Again, may I help you?"

He was one of those arrogant hippies that I loved so much, but I added to his interpretation of my ignorance by asking, "Is this the general store?" I asked like a kid told something a million times but still had to find out for sure.

His serious face widened into a smile. "Welcome, friend. You're late. There was a group through here this morning. I guess you got separated...or were you with them at all?"

So that was the password. General store. It was the code for draft dodger haven. "Uh, no. I'm alone. Am I in the right place?"

"You are. Relax. You'll be on your way tonight. We need to stagger everyone so you don't bunch up."

"Yeah, I kind of got lost." I pointed in the direction of the ridge. "The people up on the farm were kind enough to direct me here. But they weren't able to give me any food. Could I get some here? I haven't eaten for some time now."

"Sure you can." The clerk nodded repeatedly. "Rough trip, huh? Go into that room at the end of the counter." He pointed to the vacant side of the store. "There's some fruit, vegetables, and bread that was baked this morning left over from the others. I'll be in shortly."

"Hey, Clarence. How about some service down here," one of the figures around the stove yelled.

Clarence rolled his eyes and said softly, "Some of the Renaissance crowd." He turned to them and nodded. "Coming."

I watched him start toward the group, and I unavoidably glanced at them.

"Were you taken care of, man?" a bearded member in a denim vest over a black T-shirt asked. "We don't wanna cut ahead of you."

"No, no. It's OK. I'm fine." I blinked and cursed myself for not trying harder to avoid them.

"Well, that's good." He started toward me.

Clarence stopped across from the bearded muscular man. "He's in the system."

"Oh. Well, good again. Then I'll have to give him a recruitment pitch. Did you tell him who we are?"

"Just the name," Clarence said.

"I'm Snark." He slowly raised his hand as he reached me. He was taller and wider than me, and I wondered if this was a prelude to me being stomped on by all five of them.

I shook his hand and was surprised that he didn't try to break my fingers like most guys his size. "Jim," I said.

"You don't look like a runner."

"Runner?"

"Somebody headed for Canada. Why don't you join up with us? We're staying to fight them instead of dropping out like these pansies." He pointed a thumb at Clarence. "Only force can change the system, not hiding away and wishing for it."

"Force?" I looked at Snark's four comrades. "How many of you are there?"

"Hundreds. And growing every day."

"You'll excuse me, but all I've seen are farmers and peace signs. Where's this army?"

"Coming from everywhere and gathering across the river for unity." Snark yanked his thumb over his shoulder. "We only come over here to pick up some of our supplies, police the area, and look out for guys like you." He looked me over, and I felt like I was being measured for something. "You look like you've been in a few scrapes. Maybe you're a little older than the ones who usually pass through here, but you're more...seasoned than them."

Well, at last, someone who sees potential in me.

"You can use your talents with us instead of sitting around in some artist colony in Toronto complaining about the military industrial complex."

Snark was obviously more intelligent than his appearance indicated. And he would be fairly convincing if I were who he thought I was. Maybe he and his group knew something about Johnny and the others.

"You got me curious anyway. You get any more new recruits lately?" I asked.

"Why?"

"I was just wondering if there was somebody I might know in your group. Maybe guys like me passing through to Canada or…"

"There might be. We trained a lot of guys. You come on over and see."

"Let me think about it. Like, if I wanted to be trained in combat I would've let the army grab me."

"We have army personnel doing the training."

Was Red part of this group?

"You look surprised." Snark's lips parted into a thin smile that was almost hidden by his scraggly beard. "They're deserters. Guys who went through basic training and then weren't interested in going to Nam."

"Nam. You say it like you know your shit. Are you one of those who weren't interested in going?"

Snark nodded.

"I knew a guy who may have taken your route. He was from my old neighborhood. A redheaded guy who got drafted and I never heard about again. Rumors are he didn't care for army life."

"A redhead? There was one with that group that pulled in today. Yeah, and he had short hair like a military cut."

My pulse quickened. "A group of guys?"

"Yeah, they got here in a couple of passenger cars. Pretty rough roads for two-wheel-drive cars, but they made it."

Cars only? No tractor-trailer? I almost asked him if there might have been another vehicle that he failed to mention.

"They…" He stopped and came out of his reflective mood. "Look, man, you gotta come on over. I don't talk about our operations to strangers."

"Can I think about it?" My stomach growled so loud that Snark heard it. Here I was starving and I was allowing myself to be given a hard sell. "I gotta get something inside me first."

"If you're eating here, don't expect much. These fruits are vegetarians."

I chuckled to show him I got it. "All puns aside, where can I find you?"

"Like I said before, across the river. But you won't be able to get ten feet past the bridge without an escort. Why don't you just come with us now?"

Something didn't seem right. It sounded like I was going to be shanghaied and tucked away in some corner of their complex for indoctrination. How did I know I'd be allowed to find Johnny and the guys if I went now? And if I did, what would happen with me walking in on them cold with these gorillas? No, I needed a couple of hours to think. Assuming these guys that Snark described *are* my guys, I'd rather find them on my own.

"I have to eat first," I insisted. "I owe…"

"We have real food. Come on."

"Look, I came this far through their system. I owe these people the curtesy to break bread with them."

"Gratitude." Snark nodded. "I like that. It shows a sense of loyalty and that you can think for yourself. OK. You sound like you're leaning to us. I'll be back through here in about four hours. If you're here, we'll talk more."

"It's a deal."

"Good." Snark turned and rejoined his friends.

My stomach growled again, and I hurried to the doorway at the end of the counter. The back room was a spacious storeroom that smelled as fresh as the outdoors. There were bushels and boxes heaped against the back wall between a half-screen door in the center of the wall and two huge corner cupboards. The cupboards were stacked with fat homemade candles and an assortment of jars filled with brightly colored fruit preserves. The large area was even roomier by the lack of furniture. There was nothing but one twelve-foot-long picnic table with five high-back cane chairs tucked under it.

There were small baskets of tomatoes, shucked corn, apples, and other produce laid out across the table. A baking pan containing two loaves of twisted baked bread and a layer of crumbs scattered across the surface of the pan sat in the middle of the table. Snark was right. I wasn't going to get a cheeseburger and fries here, but the spread lying out before me looked like a banquet. I pulled out a chair, sat, and broke off a hunk of bread with one hand and snatched a bright red beefsteak tomato with the other. I bit and chomped on the two ingredients and imagined them as a cheeseless pizza. It was good, good, good. The seeds from the tomato squirted across the table and crumbs spit from my mouth as I tried to breathe and eat at the same time. Salt would be nice for the tomato. And some butter for the bread. No, they were good as is. They were great as is.

I slowed down after three tomatoes and a loaf of bread. I looked around for something to drink. There were empty Coke bottles lined up at the end of the table. I remembered the chest in the store. No. Wait until Snark and his boys leave. Who needs another sales pitch? I picked out a nice-sized Macintosh from one of the baskets and took a healthy bite. It was as sweet as the one Martha had given to me. It was as sweet as her. Will I still be here to see her again? There was something about her. There was her gentleness, and the unselfish deed of her giving up that apple. I had to put her out of my mind. There was Gwen to think of—and my mission. I needed to get to Johnny and Pete and the rest.

So they *were* over there, over on the other side of the river. I guessed it had to be them. But what the hell were they doing? What did they have to do with these Renaissance guys? I wasn't too intent on getting over there at this moment. I could wait until dark. If something that involved my guys, the Renaissance, and the cargo in the M37s was going to happen soon, then I'm sure Snark would be involved and he wouldn't instead be running around town like an animated Uncle Sam "I want you" poster. There was still a little time left for me to hook up, and, meanwhile, maybe I could find out more background.

I plunked the spent apple core on the baking pan and folded my arms to lean on the table. My stomach was satisfied for the moment, and my logic had convinced me that I had some time to spare. I lowered my head into my folded arms and relaxed and waited for Clarence. My eyelids fluttered, and seconds later I was asleep.

My shoulder was being shaken and nudged. I sat up and lashed out at my tormentor with a sweeping open hand.

"Easy, man. I'm just waking you." It was Clarence. "It's time for you to start out."

"Oh, wow." I rubbed my eyes and stretched. "How long did I sleep?"

"Only about four hours. You needed it, so I left you alone. There's a knapsack with some food and directions to the Canadian border over there." He pointed to the olive drab backpack hanging from a peg on one of the cupboards. "All the resisters who pass through this station get one."

"Did Snark and his guys leave?"

"Sure. A while ago."

"Of course," I said. I was still shaking the cobwebs from my brain and noticed that the ceiling lights were on. "But they're coming back soon to look for me."

"Man, those guys are a pain in the ass," Clarence said as he pulled out a chair across from me.

"They give you a hard time?"

"Always. Here, you must be tired of drinking only water." He sat and pushed a bottle of Coke in front of me. "But I'm used to them. We put up with their antics to appease them."

"Appease them?" I took a slug from the bottle. "Why?"

"Like you, we don't believe in violence and we refuse to fight anyone."

"Not even to protect yourself and your rights? Why do you think *I* won't fight?"

"Because you didn't go with Snark, so you must have turned down his proposal."

"Maybe I haven't decided yet."

"You can't even think of joining them, my friend," Clarence said. "We must tolerate them because they're our allies in the fight for peace and justice, but we must also follow our own conscience."

Oh, great. Here comes the "we need a revolution" speech.

"But we still think they're demons. We call our river Styx because it divides us from Hades."

"Why is that?"

"Let me tell you about our valley. Ten years ago that factory across the river produced chemicals. It spewed acid rain and other poisons into the air. The factory was the only means of support for this town. It was a company town completely dependent on that factory, but their poisons killed every form of plant life on that mountain."

The image of the bald mountain flashed into my mind.

"So what did the government do to the polluters?" Clarence gently bounced his fist off the table in the first display of any kind of anger I had seen from him. "They gave them a slap-on-the-wrist fine to pay and ordered them to put in controls. The owners decided the cost was going to eat into their profits, so they declared bankruptcy and moved on, probably to pollute somewhere else under a different name. The people of the town were out of work, and the valley died. Some stayed to continue to farm the land as they had before the factory was built, but most left. The roads and passages became unused and were not maintained, and eventually they were overgrown. The valley became isolated. The town was even removed from any new maps that were printed in later years. It no longer existed.

"It wasn't until our movement from the cities that this town came back to life. We reestablished it and built it back in our image, naming it Nirvana, although it still isn't found in any official records. The outside world either didn't know about us or didn't care about us. And that's how we liked it. We never reclaimed the other side of the river, just left it as a monument to the ills of capitalism."

Capitalism? I cringed. *Please don't start with the Commie rhetoric.*

"Everything was good. We used candles in the buildings and lanterns on the streets at night. We used wood stoves in the winter for warmth. We built our own brick ovens to bake and tilled the soil, getting lessons from the few farmers who had stayed. We homeschooled our children, and we were satisfied with our lives. Then they came. They started drifting into town about a year ago, at first as friends. Then, as their numbers grew and they saw that we truly believed in peace, they began taking advantage of us. They began taking instead of sharing. They established their fortress over there in hypocrisy of what that site once was. They refurbished the old generators in the factory or brought in smaller ones and *modernized* the town, charging us for their utilities and for their protection."

"Protection? What would you have to pay them with?" I asked.

"They get half our marijuana crop and a third of the other crops. They have spotters who check on how much is being grown on our farms."

"Farms? I saw only one pretty big farm. Come to think of it, they were skeptical about giving me anything to eat. They must have thought I was a spotter."

"That could be. They're very scared of being reported. We have five farms and two orchards in and around the valley. They were more than we needed to support us, with enough left over to sell at markets or in our store to travelers who happened to wander in through the only passable road."

"Sell? Capitalism?"

"No! They were the fruits of socialism. We used the money for rudimentary needs and the rest to support the Underground Railroad and donate to the peace movement."

Oh boy! "So why do you let them walk all over you?"

"There's nothing we can do. They call themselves our protectors. They feel that we should be the support and supply arm of their army. Their security services consist of not allowing us out of the valley, although most of us don't want to leave but would rather make that decision for ourselves. They also don't allow anyone other than draft resisters in or to have communication with the outside world without their approval. They wanted us to stop being part of the Underground Railroad, but that was one thing we refused to comply with and finally compromised to allow them to try to recruit whoever travels through here. Those that they couldn't convince would leave unmolested by a secret route known only to a few of us. That's why Snark approached you. We used to get post cards from the central committee in Canada each time a resister who passed through here made it safely to them. We haven't received one in weeks, even though we've processed about twenty or so resisters in that time."

"How would you get mail delivery up here? It's so remote."

"We have several post office boxes in distant towns as our mailing addresses. But now the Renaissance has their couriers picking up and censoring our mail. The only thing they let us see is useless advertisements."

I remembered how Clarence had looked down his nose at me when we first met. "Again!" I stressed, as he had, "why do you let them do this to you? How many people could they have? And what are they really doing, planning some grand strategy like they say or just making themselves comfortable at your expense?"

"We've had some of our women lured over there. Only one decided to come back."

"Decided or was allowed? Maybe they let her see only what they wanted you to know."

"I really don't know why they let her come back, but she said they have somewhere around forty permanent people with others coming in and out at regular intervals. She said they have an arsenal, rifle ranges, and one of the buildings is dedicated to making bombs."

"Making bombs?" *Is that Johnny and Pete's target?* "To kill innocent people?"

"As I said, although we don't believe in their means, they are our allies and they do as they see fit to reach the same ends."

"Who's a hypocrite now?" I stood up. "No one deserves to be killed. Isn't that what you're supposed to believe? No one. But you let a bunch of thugs rule your lives and you help support their efforts to kill innocent people.

"Just remember something, my *friend*. What's happening to you has happened in every country that the Commies or any other dictatorship has taken over. It won't be long before you're asked to produce more and keep less. And if you don't, they'll start making examples, maybe use you as targets on their rifle ranges. And why? Because you would rather lie down like a beaten dog and preach peace in your sterile little world than object to being subjugated. The only reason you're pissed at them is not for what they're doing to the rest of society but because of how they're making things inconvenient for you. Well, you and your phony peace movement can go to hell."

Clarence stood to face me. "Just who are you? You're not a draft resister. Why are you here?"

"To find some guys with the balls to fight back. I'm not gonna find any here."

"You're a spotter," Clarence said, wide-eyed. "You're one of them, here to test me." He took two steps back and his chair toppled and clattered to the floor. "I didn't...I didn't mean to call you demons. I didn't mean to..."

I grabbed my jacket from my chair back, and the flashlight in the inside pocket bounced off my knee. *Screw him! Let him think I'm one of them.* I pulled on the jacket and headed for the front door with no plan but the need for some fresh air. The lights hadn't been turned on in the empty store, and the dim light of dusk was fading quickly. I noticed that all the bushels that had been stacked against the counter were gone. *The Renaissance boys must have needed some rough-age in their diet.* There were lights now lit outside, strung along the overhangs of the buildings like holiday decorations. They ran along wires between the buildings and to the bridge, where two high-mounted spotlights illuminated the structure at each end. The factory area had some illumination as well. And there were finally people out in the street.

I headed for the open entrance and caught a glimpse of a larger group of people through the side plate glass window. It was Snark and his boys just crossing the bridge and walking toward the store. I sighed in defeat. *I guess the only way I'm getting over that river is to sign up.* I began to step out onto the walk as I watched them swagger down the street like they owned it. There were more than before. I hesitated.

Wait a minute! Was that...? You couldn't miss that pointy face. It was Lenny! He was walking alongside Snark. Damn! Did he join up with them? The two of them seemed to be compatible. What the hell was going on?

I retreated into the store. I couldn't let Lenny tell them who I was or even see me. I'd never get to see Johnny or Pete for help. I'd be dead! Either Lenny or Snark would kill me, and only Lenny would have known I was ever here.

I turned and hurried to the back room. Clarence was still standing where I had left him. He seemed to be frozen in fear over the paranoia that he had been singled out and tested.

"Look, I'm willing to forget about everything you said," I shouted, hoping it would snap him out of his trance. "I won't report you if you tell me another way over the river other than the bridge."

"Why would...you want...?"

I was gambling that the Underground Railroad route crossed the river in some secluded spot. Once across, I could try to find a way into the factory complex. "We know you send the runners across the river to get to the main road," I bluffed. I grabbed his shoulders and shook him. His granny glasses shifted and sat crooked on his nose. "Snark is about to enter your store. If he finds me still here without the information, we're both in trouble. I need that route so I can stay in good standing with Snark. Do you understand?"

"Yes, I guess. Just don't…"

I heard the thump of boots at the far end of the sidewalk. I put my index finger to my mouth for Clarence to be quiet. "I won't tell if you don't," I said in a hushed tone. "Give me the route. You can always change it once it's compromised. I didn't hear anything bad you said about the Renaissance. I'll tell them that I figured out the route myself from whatever scraps of info you unknowingly let slip. OK?"

He nodded and adjusted his glasses.

"Anyone here?" I heard Snark shout from the store.

"Out the back door and follow the rear of the buildings, turn right at the river into the woods for a hundred yards," Clarence said in a raspy whisper. "There's a…"

The clomping of heavy boots approached the storeroom and Clarence clammed up. It didn't get me across the river but I couldn't wait for the rest of the directions. I gestured for Clarence to walk toward the store and meet Snark before he reached the room, then turned and ran for the back half-screen door. It was unlocked. Clarence's steps had covered mine, and I slid out into the darkness, gently closed the door, and leaned against the building to get my bearings.

"Who were you talking to, Clarence?" Snark asked.

My pulse was racing, but I lingered and slid down to the corner post, several feet from the door but still in listening range. I wanted to hear if Clarence would give me away.

"No…No one. I was just taking my inventory aloud," Clarence said.

"Where's that runner that was here earlier?"

"He left about…about an hour ago."

"You're lying, Clarence. You know what happens to liars?"

"I swear. Please. He's gone. Look around, you'll see."

I heard the thump of boots again and quickly sprang around the corner into an alley that was formed with the next building. If I followed Clarence's route, they'd see me. There was nothing to hide behind, and the spill of light from the street brightened the entire open space. I started for the front of the alley and then stopped. There were shadows cast from the sidewalk, and puffs of bluish smoke glistened in the glow of the lights. Suddenly they were gone. The world went black.

CHAPTER TWELVE

"That goddamn number three generator shut down again," someone shouted from the sidewalk. "Anybody got a flashlight?"

Flashlight! No, get past them first before you turn it on.

Damn, I had never seen such complete blackness. There was no moonlight. I looked up as I walked and tried to approximate the distance to the front of the alley. I had never seen such an array of stars, like thousands of different-size holes poked in a velvet cloth. I could see the outlines of the buildings where no stars sparkled, and I used the void as a guide to the street. I bypassed the sidewalk of the next building and instead turned right where I thought the middle of the street would be. There were lights across the river, and the machinery hum that I had heard earlier was now louder. It was probably the other generators. The bridge lights were out.

The Renaissance group on the general store sidewalk were still yelling for a flashlight, cursing and shuffling in and out of the building in confusion. I walked about twenty feet along the dirt street before pulling the flashlight from my inner pocket and snapping it on, then moved it back and forth in front of me as I walked toward the bridge. Soft glows came from some windows on both sides of the street. Emergency candles. I guess this happens often. The shimmering flames guided my way like mini-lighthouses along a channel.

I passed through the first intersection and heard the crunching of the road surface behind me. Someone was running…toward me. Did they see my flashlight beam? Were flashlights only issued to Renaissance members? The crunching grew louder, came next to me, and then passed me. Instinctively but thoughtlessly, I swung the light toward the two dark figures.

"Thanks, man. We left ours home," one of the figures yelled. They were civilians. I broke into a trot to keep up and lit the way for all of us until they turned at the next intersection. "Thanks again," they both shouted as they sped into the dark beyond the range of the beam.

Most of the windows of this last block of the town radiated with candle glow, fuzzy rectangles of yellow against the black velvet hole-punched sky.

The same dozen or so windows in the factory buildings were lit. Shapes danced in and out of the light like a shadow box puppet show. I was at the large open approach to the bridge. The candle-lit channel was behind me, and only the factory could be used as a reference point to the bridge. I had calculated that, once I crossed, it would be another hundred yards to the buildings. I was approaching the restricted area and had to turn off the flashlight to stay hidden in the night. I slipped it back inside my jacket.

I stumbled on a hard edge and felt the road surface become firm as I stepped onto asphalt. Moving my arm up and down, I tried to find the bridge railing, hoping I didn't miss it and wind up in the river. The river was rolling gently below, splashing and lapping against the bridge supports, almost in unison with the humming generators. And it was cooler. A breeze swept by. There's the rail. I grasped it and followed its lead.

As I started across, I released my grip, finding it faster to move if I only slid my fingers along the rough iron surface. I wondered how long the blackout would last. *Oh shit! What if the lights came on while I was still on the bridge?* I thought of the scene in *Stalag 17* where the spotlights are suddenly turned on and the German barracks spy is gunned down because the guards think he is an escaping prisoner. And it would be some of my own guys, like in the movie. Lenny! And because of my deceit, Johnny and Pete and everyone would be firing machine gun bullets into my dead body. No, I made it. This feels…Yes, the end of the rail, and I stepped off the edge of the asphalt.

I acclimated my footing back to dirt. OK, a hundred more yards. I only had the length of a football field to go. Then there would be the problem of getting inside.

The bridge lights came on like a movie screen suddenly illuminating a dark theater. The coolness turned warm against my back from the intensity of the closest light, and I felt as if I was standing naked on a stage. A cheer rose from town. I leaped off the road and landed in a patch of bushes, then scampered over and behind the roadside hedge and crawled back toward the river where there was thicker foliage.

The air became cool again as I slid down the embankment, pebbles and dirt following in my wake. I dug in my heels to slow my momentum and came to a stop against a sapling trunk just short of the river. I held my breath and listened.

Music blared from the factory. It sounded like...Yes, the Rolling Stones. There was relative quiet on the town side, just some muffled loud talking and shouting in the distance, probably from the general store. The river reflected the lighting as it rippled past at a steady yet quiet and calm rate. The lights were mounted only on this side of the bridge, just over me, and it wouldn't be long before someone crossed and casually glanced over the side to see me. The bridge was too narrow for cover. There was no time to sit and analyze. I had to move on.

I sidestepped along the slope to the concrete abutment and crouched as I carefully and deliberately inched my way along the narrow ledge. I stopped on the other side and listened. There was still no one on the bridge above me. The Stones were still singing. I jumped to the bank, and a twinge of pain shot through my thighs. It was the first sign of tenderness I'd had since my nap. Overall, my legs felt stronger since I had rested.

The slope wasn't as angled as on the other side, and I managed to balance with one hand against the ground and move with one leg above the other. I slipped and pushed through small landslides until I was well past the reach of the lights. I found some shrubbery for concealment and leaned back against the grade, like pressing against a slant board. I could see the bridge and the approach from my position. No activity yet.

I began to think about the last hour and came to the conclusion that my inability to keep my mouth shut and my stupidity in letting passion instead of intellect control me had brought me to this precarious point. Only the luck of the blackout had somewhat countered my mistakes. If I hadn't blown up and chastised Clarence, I would still have my cover as a draft dodger and I would have been given my knapsack of food and directions and been sent on my merry way. I would've been across the river an hour ago, ahead of where I was now and probably explaining myself to Johnny and Pete. *The knapsack. It was still hanging on the cupboard.* What if Snark saw it? It would give Clarence away, if Clarence hadn't flipped already. I had to get to Johnny and Pete. At least I was on the right side of the river. The complex was still only a hundred yards away, but I'd never make it, not even if I scrambled to the top and made a mad dash for the buildings. Snark had said I wouldn't get ten feet past the bridge without an escort. I had to circle around through the woods and try another approach.

I tensed to push myself up and then froze. Two figures appeared on the bridge, running across from my side. They stopped at the other end and waited. One of them had a hunting rifle slung over his shoulder. Then the Snark crew appeared at the edge of town. I was sure that I was well concealed but scrunched my body as though it would make me smaller. There were seven of them, including Lenny.

"Were you guys here during the blackout?" Snark shouted.

I couldn't hear the answer but saw the two newcomers nod their heads. One of them pointed behind them to indicate their previous position. *Liars!* They would've seen me if they were anywhere near the bridge. They had been goofing off.

Snark stormed past them. I didn't hear the beginning of his sentence, but as he reached this side of the bridge, I heard: "...A runner. Get over to the crossing and check the area. When you find him, bring him to me. How many more soldiers came in since I was gone?"

"Two pickups with about twenty troops," one of the guards answered.

Snark nodded and waved them off. The duo disappeared from my view.

"The rest of you draw weapons and dry cell spotlights. Spread out through the trees down to the perimeter," Snark ordered. "Remember, I want this one alive."

Good call. Alive. It was definitely me they were about to hunt. I tensed my muscles and became perfectly still. My line of sight was hazy through the thin shrubbery, but adequate.

Only Snark and Lenny remained after the mob cleared the area. They stopped a few feet from this side of the bridge when Snark tapped Lenny's arm. Snark leaned his forearms on the railing and faced out to the river. Lenny did the same.

"Let's talk, man," Snark said. From where they stood, the acoustics of the river, its banks, the setting of the bridge—whatever it was—made his words carry, and they sounded perfectly clear to me. I closed my eyes to better concentrate. "When do we get a look at the stuff?" Snark asked.

"How many times we gotta go through this? When we get our bread," Lenny said.

"Like I asked before, how do we know we'll want to buy if we don't see the goods?" Snark asked. "How do we know you even *have* the goods?"

I opened my eyes. *Were they talking about the sarin and the AR15s? They were being sold to the Renaissance?*

"Why the hell would we come up to this God-forsaken hole for nothing? Don't worry, we got them."

"My boss thinks that maybe we should deal with Sonny. He's the guy who set this deal up with our contact."

"Never mind about Sonny. He's an intermediary, that's all. I represent our bosses. I say what goes, not Sonny." Lenny spit in the river. "And when are we gonna see this general or whatever he calls himself? We've been here almost a full day and we haven't been introduced."

"He doesn't call himself a general. He's simply, Leader of the Renaissance Army." Snark twirled his hand matter-of-factly. "He has other matters to attend to. New troops keep arriving as we speak. And he's, like, trying to dig up the rest of your payment."

"You mean you don't have all the bread we agreed upon?" Lenny stood. "You better not be jerking us around or the whole shipment gets dumped in the river."

"Don't worry, some of the troops that'll be here soon have the balance. You'd get to see the Leader to discuss matters a lot quicker if you produced a sample of your goods."

"OK, we'd be willing to produce a sample if we'd see an equal sample of cash. Tell that to your leader." Lenny flexed his elbows casually against his sides. "You tell us what kind of sample you want to see and we'll tell you how much it's gonna cost. And the rest will have to be paid for soon after that or the deal is off. We can't sit on this crap for long."

"You don't like our hospitality? OK, we'll sweeten our pot. Broads. Booze. Weed. Whatever you want, we'll provide."

"Maybe after the transaction. Right now, all we want is the green stuff. Get us an answer and let's get this thing back on track."

"I'll go talk to him now," Snark said as he stood.

"OK, come see us as soon as you find out. Man, I can't believe you took me on this *patrol*, as you called it, just to discuss our deal."

"No." Snark turned to face the river again. It looked as though he were staring right at me. Although I knew I was well hidden, I still stiffened my body to try to resemble a log or some other inanimate object. "I just thought we'd see this runner we're trying to find," he continued. "He seemed interested in you guys." He stroked his beard. "Something funny about him. Especially when he mentioned knowing a redhead in the army and you guys having a redhead with you, and with short hair. I just wanted to see if any of you guys recognized him. The redhead would've been better, but since he was somewhere else and only you were…"

"Yeah, all right already." Lenny turned his head and spit in the river again. "First off, we don't know any guys ducking the draft that don't come to us first.

We can get the right documents made and recorded so the buyer doesn't have to leave home to go to Canada. Second, I could care less about some little jerk leaving the country. That's one less asshole tying up traffic with some fucked-up demonstration while I'm trying to get somewhere."

"Well, we care. We don't need these people telling tales about our camp. The fewer who know about our gathering tonight, the better." It looked like Lenny was about to say something when Snark said, "Hey, we might be interested in buying some of those documents."

"Cash first," Lenny said. Any mention of a money deal could always change a subject or train of thought for him. "Just like for our deal now. Are we done with our chat?"

"Yeah, sure." Snark put his hand on Lenny's back to usher him toward the factory. "Only, if we find this guy we'd like to show him to you guys, especially the redhead, OK?"

"Yeah, I guess so. Red should be back in less than an hour."

Then they were gone and there wasn't any music playing. Only the hum of the generators interrupted the silence, and I figured it was time to move on.

CHAPTER THIRTEEN

The last direction Clarence had given when trying to explain the route was to make a right at the end of town and through the woods for a hundred yards. *Again with a hundred yards!* Now I'd be two hundred yards away from my goal. But I couldn't lie here in the open for too long before the search swept the riverbanks, and I couldn't skirt the road in the woods that were crawling with Renaissance. I did a quick scan of the area and, finding it clear, pushed off the ground. I stepped and slid along the riverbank for about fifty feet before it began to rise into a palisade and the river picked up speed. Whatever residual light had reached this side of the river from town was now gone. I pulled out the flashlight, snapped it on, and immediately realized that it was a beacon in the night, acting as a perfect marker. *Here I am, come and get me.*

I turned it off and unscrewed the base. Military flashlights have lenses of different tints and optical textures stored in a lower compartment. I took out the red lens, replaced the cap, and placed the lens in the light socket. The red-tinted beam gave limited vision of the ground as I walked, but it was almost undetectable and better than flying blind.

I picked my way through the underbrush and zigzagged between the trees until I came upon a small clear strip along the cliff line. After assessing about how far I had come since being lined up with the rear of town, I began to pace, each stride a yard, to determine the distance to the end of Clarence's directions. I had gone about seventy paces when I saw a glint of light ahead of me. I shut off my flashlight and hurried back into the concealment of the trees.

A light beam ricocheted off the trees around me as it swung through the forest. It swept past the thick trunk I hid behind and became a long steady streak as it pointed away from the river.

"Nobody's around here," a voice shouted from ahead. "Let's get out'a here." It was probably the liars from the bridge. "We can join up with the other guys on the perimeter."

Branches snapped, leaves rustled, and twigs crackled under foot as the light beam moved deeper into the forest until it became a distorted circle that grew smaller and finally disappeared. I waited a few minutes to be sure no one doubled back or stayed to guard the area, then moved forward again.

I wouldn't have to pace out the remaining yards. I just headed for where the duo had made their search. The palisade continued to rise, and when it leveled out it was about twenty feet above the river. There appeared to be an obstruction across the width of the now-raging river. I couldn't see much detail with the red lens, so I replaced it with the clear lens. I waited another few minutes, listening for any sound of the forest being disturbed. There was nothing but the rushing water lapping against the obstruction, so I snapped the light back on.

I shone the beam over the river and saw a steel ledge running bank to bank, two other small beams below it, and the remains of a concrete wall jaggedly protruding from the other bank. This must have been a dam once. I swung the beam back and saw the remnants of a building in front of me. It was old and constructed of fieldstone and weathered barn board. It was nestled into the cliff, and one wall extended down to the water line. There was a large opening in the wall.

I grabbed onto a hefty tree limb and leaned out over the edge to shine the light into the gaping hole. There were cogs and gears, levers and rods, all rusted and locked in place. It was either an old water mill or a small hydroelectric project at one time. I studied the steel ledge. It was solidly embedded at both ends and was wide enough for someone to walk across without feeling nervous. This was the crossing.

I leaned back and saw a path traveling from the ledge, past the building, and into the forest. The bypassing of the Renaissance restricted area. But the Renaissance soldiers were here patrolling the area. Hadn't Snark ordered them to *check the crossing*? They already knew the runner's route.

In my concentration on the structures I wasn't watching my step. I stumbled on something soft but caught hold of a branch to steady myself. I shone the light at the ground. It was a knapsack like the one in the storeroom. The back of the bundle looked like it had holes in it. I lifted it and turned it over. There were larger holes with ragged edges punched from inside and covered with a reddish brown stain. Maybe the apples and tomatoes had...*My God!* It wasn't apple or tomato juice. It was blood! One of the runners was wearing this on his back and he was gunned down. *Damn!* I dropped the backpack like it was contaminated and, although the blood was dry, wiped my hand on my dungarees.

Where was the person that had worn this knapsack? Where was his body? And if the Renaissance knew the route, they must have taken out the other two or three that came through today. And maybe even the twenty or so that Clarence said came through in recent weeks. Where were their bodies? Damn, these Renaissance guys are nothing but murdering sons of bitches.

My stomach churned. *Damn. Damn.* This was not good. Maybe I didn't like what these runners were doing, but it wasn't a reason for them to be killed. I suddenly felt sorry for them, for their families, and for their friends waiting in vain for them to arrive. This was not what they deserved. What irony. They were running from a war, from the possibility of being killed. What a bitch, man. What a bitch.

Then I realized that it could've been my blood on that knapsack if I had continued to masquerade as a runner. Maybe my journey wasn't as smooth as I'd like, but somehow, for some reason, I was being guided and I was being spared. I hoped it would last just a little longer, just long enough to reach Johnny and Pete so they could answer my questions about dealing instruments of death to a pack of savage murderers.

I walked to the side of the abandoned building and found the open entrance, hoping I wouldn't find the bodies stacked inside like a cord of firewood. I reluctantly shone the light inside and saw that the single large room contained only the carcass of what appeared to be a stripped generator. The main shaft from the riverside wall and the frame and mounts were rusted and laced with cobwebs. It had probably been used to supply some of the power to the town during its heyday and was then stripped by the original factory operators or the Renaissance for parts. There was nothing else in the shell of the building.

I stepped outside, snapped off the flashlight, and listened again for any movement. Crickets. There was a slight wind in the treetops and the heavy torrents of water rushing below. OK, no one around. But if I took this path it wouldn't be long before I ran into a Renaissance patrol and maybe took a bullet or two from them. Snark's orders were to take me alive but I wasn't up for that either, especially if it was Lenny who verified who I was. And what if one of these guys didn't give a crap about orders? What if they wanted to continue their target practice? I had to move downriver.

I crossed to the far side of the building before I turned on the flashlight. If I kept it facing down and shielded from the side by my other hand, it would be less likely to be seen from the woods, and I wouldn't have to use the hindering red lens. The small strip of clearing along the cliff became narrow and was capped with flat boulders and rock ledges jutting out over the edge. I continued along.

This was getting frustrating. First it was a hundred yards. Then it was two hundred yards, and by now I must have traveled another hundred yards. I'll be back in New York before long. There was nothing in front of me but more trees, rocks, and the river below. The underbrush along the forest floor became impassable. I couldn't veer into the woods any longer, even if I had wanted to. I was getting tired again. I sat on a smooth flat boulder and dangled my feet over the edge of the cliff.

What the hell had I gotten myself into? I could be home watching television or with Gwen in Poughkeepsie, content to know I wasn't a hero and not giving a crap whether I'd choose flight or fight. Instead, I'm sitting here alone in the dark with people wanting to love me, recruit me, or kill me. Great choices. My clear choice would've been to stay with Martha, if I were rational and normal and not on some ridiculous quest. It would be for only a short time, just to talk and to feel like I was with Gwen. I'm sure both of them had the same general outlook on life, only in different age brackets and environments. I would feel at home and I would relax. Then afterward, I'm sure I'd be right back here sitting in the dark, trying to find a way to the end of the trail I had chosen to follow.

I swept the flashlight beam across the river, and the waves and white caps danced through the circle of light. I aimed it at the opposite shore and then down along the bank I sat on. At first I thought it was part of a rock formation projecting from the cliff, but it was smooth and straight edged. Concrete. There was something man-made sticking out of the side of the cliff.

CHAPTER FOURTEEN

I stood and moved back to the spot above the object. It looked like the edge of a sewer pipe, and it protruded about two feet from the rock wall. I wondered...Yeah, I'll bet it leads to somewhere in the factory complex. I surveyed the rock ledges leading down to the pipe. I had to take the chance. If fate led me here, it was to find this way instead of wandering aimlessly through the forest.

A crooked random ladder of narrow ledges and flat stones led down the palisade to the pipe bottom. I tried to memorize the pattern of the steps before turning out the flashlight and tucking it inside my jacket, then zipping up. I couldn't lose my only weapon against the darkness.

The blackness surrounded me again as I grasped a hold between rock gaps and started my decent into the abyss. It was about fifteen feet to the bottom of the conduit. I slid my foot along the face of the cliff and probed for a stepping-stone. Got it. Now get a grip on a lower rock. Next foot. Probe. Footing. Keep that body tight against the side. Gravity was still down there ready to pull me into the river. Slide. More. This is a long step as I remember. Stretch. The river sounded even louder and angrier in the dark. Got it. Move your hand down. Use that crevasse for a grip. Good. Now stop and rest.

I felt around the wall to my side and found that my waist was about even with the top of the pipe. I tried to swing my foot into the opening, but the concrete lip was too far from the plane of the wall to allow easy access. A couple more steps would do the trick. One. Grip. Twooo. My foot slipped. The rocks at this level were wet from the river spray. My fingers ached as I fought to maintain my hold on a craggy rock above my head. I tried to get a firm foothold again but slipped, and this time my grip released.

I swung my arm and then my leg inside the concrete lip as I started to slide and pushed hard. My body arched sideways into the mouth of the pipe, hanging in space for an instant before gravity sucked me down and in. I twisted as I fell and landed heavily on my butt, just catching about six inches of the lip, facing out toward the river. I threw my upper body backward and the back of my head bounced off the concrete. I came to rest with my legs still dangled over the lip. I lay there, gasping for breath, shaking, and feeling cold. The spray was soaking my sneakers and socks. I wished I were with Gwen. I rose up on my forearms and slid my entire body into the pipe, raising my feet against the side curve.

After a minute, confirming I was still alive, I sat up and pulled out the flashlight. The height of the pipe was about five feet. I stood and bent forward to fit. The tunnel ran back beyond the range of the light beam, but from what I could see, it looked dry and fairly intact. There were a few cracks with small tree roots weaving through. Whatever this tunnel had been used for was long ago retired, and I was sure the mouth of the tunnel being this far downriver and away from town was purposely so the general public wouldn't see whatever crap it had been dumping into the river. It was about to become a rural subway buried beneath a forest.

I started forward, following the light beam and feeling a slight dampness in my shoes. It was a good thing I wore laced sneakers. Loafers would be floating miles down the river by now. My gait was flat-footed from bending over and compensating for the curvature of the footing. The tunnel ran straight and at a slight upward incline. I guessed it was parallel to the factory road and that it would have to start into a bend soon. The air became stale and cold the deeper I traveled. My back was beginning to ache. My feet were cold.

The light beam began to refract along the surface of the tube. The passage was bending, beginning its turn toward the factory. It was a smooth, steady turn, rather than a radical ninety degrees, and when it was completely shifted to a direction perpendicular to the factory, the angle of rise was a little more obvious. There was something ahead. Damn, it was a break in the concrete. The entire right side of the tunnel was gone and replaced by a landslide of dirt interwoven with webs of roots snarling the passage. The roots were everywhere along the floor of the tube, spreading within and from the pile of dirt that all but blocked my way. The roots looked like crawling vipers by the light and shadows cast from the concrete walls and earth blockage. It looked like a snake pit.

I stopped at the wall of dirt and shone the light through the two-foot by two-foot space along the open left side. It was clear past the landslide. I couldn't see any remnants of the concrete that had collapsed, and I guessed it was buried under the expanse of soil that now formed the floor of the eight-foot-long dirt tunnel. I was weary of crawling through it. The earth from the forest outside and above could begin to flow again and cause a cave-in. My family had been coal miners in their youth, and I remembered the stories told of cave-ins and how they buried men alive and you would be sucking dirt into your nose and mouth, trying to get just one more breath of air. *Stop!* I had to go through it.

Holding the flashlight ahead of me, I started a crawl that resembled a swimmer's dog paddle. The cool soft dirt sank in spots but then firmed, reinforced by the root system like rebar in cement, before softening again. Anytime I hit a soft patch I would sink slightly and the displacement would activate a spill of dirt from the side. I wanted to move faster, to get the hell out, but stayed cautious of that extra dirt shifting down and around me. I was halfway through when the floor began to give more often and I would have to kick away the falling dirt to keep it from covering my legs. I was digging and crawling with every movement. Faster. I had to get out. The air was thin, and I gasped as I plowed ahead. Panic was getting a grip. Get going. I summoned all the strength of my legs and sprang forward. It was like trying to run on a beach. I was beginning to get light–headed, but I was near the edge of the dirt. I reached out and grabbed a substantial hunk of root. It held firm and, with a final flex of thigh and calf muscles, I yanked my legs free and tumbled over the dirt floor to the root-covered concrete floor. A shower of earth followed and momentarily pinned me against the roots.

I pulled myself free and stumbled along the conduit until I was sure I was out of danger. I crouched, looked back, and saw that the redistribution of earth had elongated and shrunk the dirt passage. There was still a hole, but it looked much more dangerous as an escape route, and I hoped I wouldn't have to retreat from what was ahead. I caught my breath, inhaled a few more times, and found that the air seemed a little sweeter on this side.

I stood again, dusted the loose dirt from my clothing and hair, hunched to fit in the confined space, and continued on. The scraping of my soles echoed and sounded like someone doing a choo-choo impression for a baby. I began to feel a flow of fresher but slightly tainted air. There were still minor cracks in the structure of the tunnel, but nothing appeared ahead that seemed a hindrance. Then the flashlight beam pulled something out of the darkness. It was a fork. The split tunnels branched off at forty-five degree angles. When I reached the junction I saw that there was light farther down the left tunnel. The end of the other was dark and longer than the beam could reach.

I tried the left tunnel. It was about a hundred feet long, and I saw that the light came from a series of overhead grates. I turned off the flashlight in case there was someone nearby above me, and I peered through the first grate. The starry sky was above. I tried to lift the grating, but it wouldn't budge. I looked from whatever angle I could manage and made out red brick buildings on both sides probably separated by a courtyard, which I was under. There were outside spotlights at intervals along the building fronts. I couldn't see anyone but heard muffled sounds of laughing, shouting, and music playing. There was a party going on that competed with the constant buzz of the generators.

I moved to the next grate and tried to lift it. It was either too heavy or frozen in place. The third was the same. I looked out the metal grille and saw the base of one of the chimneys on the roof of the building across the yard. I was definitely in the heart of the complex. I did my Groucho Marx walk to each of the grates and found all of them unmovable. This branch of the tunnel system must have been—or could still be—a storm drain.

I backtracked under the grating, turned on the flashlight at the junction, and started down the other tunnel. There was a rancid odor like acid fumes in the air but no signs of dampness or stains, so it was probably a lingering stench that had permeated some of the porous sections of the concrete. This branch was longer and narrower than the other. I was pushing myself along with my free hand as I walked when I reached a dead end and found double steel doors barring the way. I swung the light around the area and found that the steel barrier was the only indication of an opening or portal. There didn't appear to be any lock mechanism, so the doors were probably secured on the other side.

There was a small space between the steel plates. I put the flashlight down and wedged my fingers into the opening. I flexed my muscles and tugged. The right door creaked and heaved back in my hands. The damn thing wasn't locked or in need of any muscle at all.

Only a trace of light trickled from the other side of the doorway, along with the faintest hint of the same mixture of music and voices I had heard in the other tunnel. The stench that filled the tunnel was now more pungent but bearable. I still had to cough a few times and spit to get the taste out of my mouth. Whatever had flowed through this system had definitely been caustic. I surmised that the odor was less intense or not detectable at all in the main tube because water mixed with the mystery solution at the junction and diluted it.

I didn't try the other door. There was enough space to squeeze through. I passed into the inner concrete chamber and noted that the other door's locking control rods ran up to somewhere in the darkness above. I stood straight and took pleasure in stretching the kinks out of my back. I wondered how gorillas and people with back problems could walk around like that all day long. I shook some loose dirt from my clothes and hair and wiped some of the clay soil from my hands onto my jeans.

I shone the flashlight beam up the walls and around the chamber. The enclosure I stood in was a ten by ten vat or pool that climbed about fifteen feet high. A steel ladder ascended the wall just past the door control rods. I heard a dripping sound and flicked the beam on the wall. There was a puddle of fluid on the ground at the base of the wall. It looked red, and it was dripping from a flange or lip at the top of the wall. *Damn!* More blood? Could it be from…?

Whatever it was, I sure as hell couldn't go back, so I started up the ladder to confront it. I was almost to the brink when I twisted awkwardly and tried to point the flashlight above to see how much farther. One of the rungs suddenly snapped under my foot. As I instinctively grabbed the rung over my head with both hands, the flashlight sailed down into the vat. I heard it shatter and plastic shards bounce and clink-clink-clink below. I moved my feet up another step and paused in memorial. I could've cried in frustration, having lost an old friend who had been with me every step of the journey. But there was a trace of light above, and thankfully I was now inside the complex.

I moved slowly and more deliberately up the remainder of the ladder, then grabbed the lip around the perimeter to pull myself to the floor of the room. The windows were opaque and only allowed enough light to make out occasional dark shapes and their shadows.

At the end of the room was a transom window, the kind that was usually over entrance doors in older buildings. I started toward it and then sensed something in front of me. I stretched my arms out and walked into a smooth-textured object. When it swung away from me, I realized it was hanging from the ceiling. There was a grinding squeal and a bumping sound. Then the blurred shadow swung back through my arms and struck me in the face and chest. Again I felt the smoothness of skin and then ribs before it began its back swing away from me. *My God.* It was a naked body. I spun away from it in terror, and it swayed erratically until it slapped into whatever was hanging alongside it. The grinding and squealing of metal on metal were followed by slapping sounds, the sounds of naked bodies colliding. I remembered the blood in the vat, and then I knew my fears had been real. It was the runners, their naked bodies hanging from ceiling hooks.

I let out a low moan, and panic shot a charge of adrenaline to my legs as I stumbled forward. I pushed at the bodies as I ran to keep them from slamming into me. My stomach juices began to churn upward, and my breath came shallow and loud. I panted and bellowed in a baritone gurgle like people do when calling for help to wake from a nightmare. Then I heard a sharp snap and felt something bony tangle in my legs. I fell forward and sprawled in front of the door below the transom.

I sprang to my feet and grabbed the knob. I didn't care who might be on the other side of the door. I had to get out. I pushed hard, gasping in panic when I found it wouldn't open. Was it locked? *No.* The door swung in, and fresh air and bright lights blasted me in the face. A spotlight shone from across the open court-yard directly in my eyes, blinding me for a moment. I turned back and saw the pieces of bone on the floor, funny-looking pointy bones—and a rib cage. My eyes adjusted. *You idiot!* They're antlers.

I leaned on the jam and pushed the door fully open. The spot from across the way highlighted the gauntlet I had just ran. Slabs of meat still swayed in circular or lateral motions from steel eyehooks. They were deer carcasses, skinned and dressed. The stomach juices subsided and I found I didn't need to vomit after all. Then I shuddered as I thought about what my imagination had conjured up while escaping the supposed aftermath of the Renaissance cannibalism and depravity. Oddly, I was relieved to know they were only common murderers and not demented ogres, and doubly glad because I was now inside their fortress.

CHAPTER FIFTEEN

From what I could see in the swatch of light running down the middle of the room, the building was only used as an *animal* slaughterhouse and butcher shop. The deer were probably hunted in the surrounding woods and prepared here and then moved to some refrigerated storage. *Just like Robin Hood and his Merry Men. Or more appropriate to here, merry murderers.*

I looked at the broken antlers that I had tripped over and smiled. What a jerk. I had accused Clarence of being paranoid, and here I am panicking over deer carcasses. *But there were still human bodies somewhere.*

I stepped into the courtyard, closed the door, and moved into the shadows of an alcove to scan the scene. I didn't see any movement in the moderately lit area. The yard was almost a quarter of a mile long by half that distance wide and was composed entirely of cobblestone. It was surrounded by the dull red-brick factory buildings and sloped toward the middle five grates I had seen from their underside. The sides of the grates were individually ringed with concrete, obviously why I wasn't able to open them.

The building I had just left stood with two more similar one-story structures lined after it to the rear of the yard. The hum of generators came from one of those buildings. There were about two dozen motorcycles parked outside a two-story unlit building that dominated the rear boundary. A fifty-foot enclosed breezeway connected it and the main three-story factory across from me. The three towering smokestacks occupied the rear corner of the factory, and one of the stacks emitted a slight whiff of smoke that was being swept away by the upper winds. The walls of the building had occasional rectangles of newer, brighter red brick where unwanted window spaces had been plugged. The main building ran the entire length of the courtyard, and most of its eight-foot multipaned windows on the second floor and a few on the ground floor were lit. Both the sounds of more generators and the party came from there. Another six Harleys sat near tall, double wood-and glass-paned doors near the center of the building. This appeared to be the main entrance.

The end of the courtyard that bordered the road had a wide brick and cinder block archway that was molded into and flanked by buildings housing loading docks. A double wrought-iron picket gate blocked off the entrance. I thought I saw movement outside the gate along the road, but then it was still again. There were a variety of vehicles, totaling ten, parked at the right-hand loading platform.

Only a red and white Chevy was parked in front of the other. It had a dent in the right front fender. The Buick wasn't there, but I was now sure that some of my guys were. I only hoped they were the right guys. There was light behind the long, shaded picture window of the loading dock behind the Chevy. They were either there or at the party, living it up with their new friends. *That was uncalled for!* But what could I think until I had some more facts?

Well, the only way to find out who was behind that window was to hope the shade wasn't completely drawn and to look. I scanned the area again and took one step before the movement I thought I had seen before returned. The entrance gates swung open, with a guard on each pushing them until there was room for a dark-colored van to pass into the courtyard. The van backed into the last open parking space at the right loading platform as the guards pulled the heavy iron gates closed. The guards disappeared just as the seven occupants of the van emerged from its opened doors. They were laughing boisterously as they followed each other through the main entrance doors of the party building. A minute later, a cheer rang out from the building, obviously welcoming the newcomers.

I waited for five minutes before starting toward the Chevy again and was about halfway when one of the double main doors opened. There wasn't nearby cover to slip into, so I turned up the collar of my jacket, hunched forward with my hands in my pockets, and kept walking like I belonged.

It was only one person, a woman. She closed the door, lit up a cigarette, and started across the courtyard. Her high heels clicked on the stones as she walked slowly on an intersecting path with mine. She was flashy, with dark hair teased into a bouffant and lots of makeup and a tight red miniskirt. She was probably one of the Renaissance chicks.

After my quick inspection, I turned forward and tried to ignore her. I kept veering toward the Chevy but saw that she was heading for the same point.

"Hello, stranger," she said.

I couldn't believe my ears. I stopped and looked at her.

"So you are here," Martha said.

"What the hell…?" I started walking again, feeling uneasy, unable to cope with what was happening, and uncertain of who else might show up at the gate or come through the same doorway.

She followed, flicking the cigarette away. I reached the Chevy and stopped. I wanted to get a look through that window, but I was suddenly overwhelmed with the need to see what had brought about this metamorphosis. I leaned against the quarter panel in the shadow of the loading dock, feeling it was dark enough to screen me. She slinked toward me like a hooker. My shock turned to disappointment and was probably registered on my face.

"Surprised?" she asked as she stopped in front of me.

"You might say that. I mean…" I couldn't find any words and only held my palms out, baffled.

"I've been looking for you," she said with a sultry smile. "I thought you said we would get together tonight."

"I was kind of busy. How did you know I'd be here?"

"Well, when I came looking for you and found Clarence out behind the store like he was in a daze, mumbling about the Renaissance and the resister who was really one of them, I figured he meant you."

"So you got all dolled up to come over here to find me?"

"That's right. I knew there was a major party tonight and that if you were one of them, you'd be here."

"I still don't understand the change in appearance…and, it looks like, attitude. I saw you as a sweet country girl with convictions and your own kind of morality. You…"

She threw her head back and laughed. "That's what I'm supposed to be in front of my brother and the others. In fact, he got mad at me for mentioning free love to you, a stranger, even though he believes in it, too. But when I'm over here, this is my persona."

"Well, you just made a big mistake, honey. Your farm girl image is what had won me over. The way you look now I can find for a dime a dozen at Times Square."

"OK, I'll change back. That's how I am most of the time, the way you want me to be. You'll see." She touched my cheek. "Your face is dirty. What have they got you doing?"

I pushed her hand away. "So you've been here before, to other parties?"

"Yes…but I don't like doing it. I only come here to find someone to take me away. Someone like you, who isn't a rough obnoxious beast that lies and only wants one thing and once he's had it laughs when you ask him to get you out of this goddamn…" She started sobbing and pushed into me. In heels, she was still a head shorter. "I can't take it anymore."

"Watch it, my clothes are filthy." I started to push her away, but she felt so comforting pressed against me. I was weary and vulnerable. I put my hands on her waist. "I thought you were happy here. I mean, as a farm girl."

"No, I was happy in East Elmhurst. My kid brother and his friends heard about this valley and decided to migrate here. The only other family we have is an older sister. She's had a few nervous breakdowns through the years and was ready for another when our brother told us what he was going to do. She wanted to keep what was left of the family close by. I made a promise to her that I'd look out for him. I followed and would regularly get word back to her that we were OK. It gave her hope and stability knowing we would someday return.

"I couldn't convince my brother to leave, and when I was ready to pack up, the Renaissance showed up and virtually shut us off from the outside. They don't want anyone knowing they're here or what they're planning."

"You know what they're planning?"

"Only that it's something big. The Leader was bragging to everyone how this weekend they were going to change things for the better. That's why they call themselves the Renaissance, because they are going to enlighten and change our society."

"And you believe that?"

"Well…I know there's a lot of them showing up tonight, a lot more than have ever been here before, and they already had weapons and explosives stored here and probably things I haven't seen."

"So you're the one Clarence said came back?"

"Yes. I couldn't stay here. Even though I was fed up with my place on the farm, I was needed there with my brother. But the guards know me. They let me pass—only as far as here and never beyond. I sneak over as an occasional diversion. Are you with this new group?" She stepped back and looked at the loading dock.

"Yes."

"I thought so. That's why I was on my way here."

"Me being your last resort?"

"Oh, no. It's not like that. I was on my way here to…" She looked away. "To, uh…"

"To entertain the troops and find someone you could make your pitch for freedom to, whether it was me or whoever is in there?"

"No! I really did come to specifically find you, and I don't care for your judgment of me." She backed off another step. Her mascara-coated eyes squinted, and her small face pouted from behind the makeup. There were no streaks from her crocodile tears. "You're not being who I thought you were, either."

"I think I've had about enough of this fairy tale about sisters with breakdowns and a trip to the country to work on a farm." I pushed off the car and swung around her. "I'd like to get away from this damn place, too."

"Then take me with you." She grabbed my arm from behind as I started for the platform steps. "Please. I'll do anything."

"I'm sure you would." I pulled loose and started up the stairs. "But I can't seem to find any trust for a party girl who has a one-track agenda."

I had to get a look in that window. I really didn't care if Lenny were there, just as long as Johnny or Pete were also there to back me. Even if they didn't back me, I had come through enough shit to get here. I was going to join them, even if it were the last thing I did.

"Please!" she screamed.

"Quiet, will you? The guards might…" I heard movement inside the room. As I reached the platform, Martha grabbed a handful of my jacket and pulled herself to the platform with me. I reached back, snatched her arm, and yanked her around to my side. "OK, you want something from me? You better be prepared to give something in return."

"Yes, of course. Wait a minute. Like what?"

I half-turned at the sound of a lock mechanism snapping and was facing the door that bordered the window. It swung in. I froze in place and probably looked like the proverbial deer-in-the-headlights to Red, because that's what he looked like to me. We both stared in silence at our mirror images for a few seconds until I said, "We're your neighborhood welcoming committee. May we come in?"

I tightened my grip on Martha's arm and pulled her past Red, who had stepped backward into the room. Her short hesitant steps sounded like castanets as her high heels clicked on the cement platform.

We entered what resembled a dormitory room with two couches and four variously styled chairs pushed against two of the whitewashed cinder block walls. A fifties art deco lamp barely lit the room from a rear corner. Empty beer bottles, bags of snacks, and paper plates littered an antique but battered dining room table in the middle of the bare, unpolished wooden floor. Johnny and Pete were just rising from two of the armchairs. There was no one else in the room. *No Lenny.*

"Yes, it's me," I said as I jerked Martha even with me. "And this is my lovely assistant for the evening."

Johnny and Pete looked at each other and then back to me.

"Well, I'll be damned," Pete said. "I don't know why I'm surprised, but how the hell…?"

"It wasn't easy."

Red closed the door and moved around in front of us. "Who's your friend?"

I realized I was still holding Martha's arm. I released my grip and put my hand gently on her back. "This is Martha. She helped me today, and she needs a ride back to New York."

"Oh! Thank you." She puckered and leaned toward me. A pang of guilt must have made me think of Gwen. I turned my cheek to Martha and she kissed it, pulling back with a puzzled look. She turned to the others. "I hope you can help me."

"Well, I don't know," Johnny said, "We'll see what we can do." He turned to Pete again, nodded, and then faced me. "Can I see you back here?"

I followed Johnny into the rear of the room. There were two unmade beds, a refrigerator, and two doors along the unpainted plasterboard far wall. Different-colored duffle and canvas travel bags were piled in a corner. Johnny opened one of the doors and stepped into a cold, dark room that, by the echo of our steps, appeared to continue for a long distance past the reach of the light. There were wooden and cardboard boxes, with the names of their contents blacked out, stacked near the doorway.

"Why the hell did you bring that girl here?" he asked softly.

"She followed me home."

"You and those damn wisecracks." He pushed on my chest until I was beyond the doorway and then partially closed the door until only a sliver of light shone on the side of his face.

"Just trying to be me. I know it's a shock to have me waltzing in here out of the blue. I just wanted…"

"Yeah, you're here. Didn't I warn you? What if Lenny were also here right now? He's going to find out about you sooner or later."

"Not unless one of you guys tells him." I paused, but he didn't respond. "By the way, where are he and the other guys?"

"None of your business. You have no rights here. No rights to ask questions and no rights to my protection. You have nothing to offer. You're an extra burden and another problem because you have no idea what our situation is."

"Such as selling poison gas and assault rifles to some crazy bastards?"

Johnny's jaw dropped. He stared at me for a few seconds. "How did you know that? Just how the hell *did* you get here?"

"I won't lie to you, Johnny. I hid out in your trailer and hitched a ride. I got out a little too early and couldn't find you until now."

"You goddamn magnificent bastard." He tried to smile. "What am I gonna do with you? You're like a bulldog. Only, you locked your jaws around something you're gonna regret."

"What do you mean?"

"We were supposed to get our money and be out of here today, but now they've put us off until later tonight before they say they can come up with our dough."

"I know."

"How the hell do you know so much?" Johnny asked, his face expressing his disbelief at my statement.

"I really do know. I happened to be in the right places at the right time."

"Well, your streak just ended. You're now in the wrong place at the wrong time." His facial muscles loosened, and I could tell by his voice that he was slowly accepting my application for reinstatement. "I don't know why they're stalling, but we're not going anywhere until they come up with our dough and the deal is finalized."

"Still with the deal, huh? I can't believe you guys would do something like this. How can you sell crap like that to a bunch of cruds looking to start a revolution or something, to probably the very bastards who killed Madge?"

"Don't start your moralizing with me." His face tightened again. "The wheels are in motion and we wouldn't care if they were from Moscow. Money is the name of this game, and it'll be played until the final out."

"And Red," I slipped in. I almost felt betrayed as an American. "How can a lieutenant in the army be a party to this?"

"Just remember one thing," Johnny said, unmoved. "You helped deliver the goods and you were paid for your time. You're both legally and morally involved in this just as much as we are."

"Money?" I had forgotten about the twenties in my upper jacket pocket. I reached in and plucked out the folded bills. "I didn't know what was in those trucks then. You can't hang a guilt trip on me. I don't want this blood money." I flipped them on the floor. "I'm buying back my dignity and peace of mind."

"Too late. You wanted in? Well, you're in, and you're responsible for your actions just like we are for ours. Once payment for the goods is handled, we're done with our work. We take our pay and then we do what we have to do." Johnny bent down and picked up the five twenties. "*You* do your job, you get paid…and then you do what you have to do." He stared deep into my eyes as he handed me the bills.

There was more to be done. They weren't here just for the money. And I was going to be part of it. "I…understand." I took the bills and slid them into my pants pocket, but I would probably give them to Martha, or to charity, to somehow keep my involvement pure.

"Good." He patted my arm. "You know something? You stink. You smell like you've been crawling around in a sewer."

"As a matter of fact, I have. I'll tell you later. Can I get a shower and change of clothes?"

"Forget about a shower. You get a bar of soap and a sink like the rest of us. This isn't exactly a four-star hotel. I'll give you the shirt and pants I was going to use as a change. You need it more than me." He pointed at me. "But don't think you're gonna get my clean underwear. That's where I draw the line."

I laughed and we stared at each other for a moment, then grasped each other's shoulder and shook hands.

"I'm really glad to see you," Johnny said. "I tried my best to keep you out of this, but you being you, it's like trying to piss up a rope. What Pete and I did back there at the club was to keep you out of harm's way. It was to appease Benny and Kelly. I had a feeling it wouldn't do much good, and now that you're here, you'll have to pull the same weight as everyone else. I'll keep Lenny in check. I'm sure he wouldn't take the chance of blowing this trip by going after you."

I thought about telling Johnny of the incident at the warehouse, of Lenny's threat, but I didn't want to sound like a wimp looking for protection. I would face what was in store but would stay close to Johnny nevertheless.

"Pete and I were talking before about the strange feeling we both had that you were close by. That's why we weren't completely surprised to see you."

"Sure, like the Corsican Brothers. The three of us are always somewhere along the same wavelength. Look, now that you tell me you're having trouble with these guys, maybe Martha can help your situation. She's a little schizoid, but she knows her way around this place."

"So do we. Red went off alone on scouting missions and secretly explored most of the buildings. We don't expect any trouble, but if anything happens, we'll be ready."

"So should we tell her to take a powder?"

"Not right away. I don't know how she'll react. She might go crying to the drunks across the way and start trouble. You go clean up and change. We'll see if we can get anything useful out of her for now." Johnny opened the door and ushered me back into the dorm room. "That other door is the bathroom. I'll slip the clothes to you."

Martha had made herself comfortable on one of the couches. Red sat on a chair pulled in front of her. She was purring something I couldn't hear, and it was obvious that she was flirting with him. Pete sat on the other couch, smiling and listening to her pitch. I shook my head and entered the bathroom.

The room reminded me of the men's room at our neighborhood bar. A toilet bowl and a sink with a lower cabinet were squeezed into a four-by-four space, and a bare lightbulb hung from the ceiling. I stripped off my jacket, shirt, and undershirt.

Johnny returned with the clothes. "I think you brought us a gem. Red is falling in love." He smiled and closed the door.

I washed, changed, and used the toilet. I had cleaned off the jacket as best as I could and slung it over my arm. I balled up my dirty clothes, transferred the money and other contents to the pockets of the chinos I was wearing, and tossed the pile into the cabinet under the sink for storage. I almost felt like a human being again when I stepped back into the main room. Pete was standing at the refrigerator, and when he saw me he closed the door with his elbow. He had two bottles of beer in one hand and a single bottle in the other. He handed the single bottle to me.

"Man, just what I need." I took the bottle and followed him to the seats. Johnny was sitting on one of the cushioned armchairs. Red and Martha were gone, and Johnny saw my puzzled look.

"They're taking a walk around the compound so Martha can scope out what Red doesn't already know about the place," Johnny said. "So they say."

"Yeah," I said as I sat on a high-back chair. My fantasy about the sweet innocent girl working in the fields had just about faded from my thoughts. Welcome back, Gwen. "He better not tell her he's military or he'll get a kick in the nuts instead of a piece of ass."

I took a slug of beer. It wasn't very cold, but it tasted good after a few days of abstinence. "So where's the rest of the guys?"

"You first," Johnny said. "Since it's just us, tell us what happened between the time we last saw you and when you walked in here."

I detailed my trek for them, polishing off a second beer and two large bags of potato chips, occasionally stopping to chuckle with Johnny and Pete as they marveled at my exploits. I felt back at home, back where I belonged. "So where's the other guys?" I asked again.

"As you can see, the trailer and everything in it are somewhere else," Johnny said. "We have everything stashed away in a secret spot out in the woods. We each take a two-hour shift guarding it. We don't think they'll find it, but it's best to be careful." Johnny looked at his watch. "Lenny and Sonny should be back any minute now. Lenny drove the Looneys there to relieve Sonny. You know the Looneys—inseparable—so they're pulling a double watch together."

"That was some bumpy ride the trailer took," I said. "Wasn't there a more direct, smoother route?"

"The only paved road that comes anywhere near here is up a winding mountain road. Nothing over twenty, twenty-five feet long can make the sharp turns. And we didn't want to be spotted by some local sheriff or state cop."

"Sonny sure battered the hell out of it on those narrow trails. Whose rig is it?"

"It belongs to Lenny's uncle. He put in a stolen vehicle report this morning, as soon as Lenny let him know it would never be found again."

"I didn't hear that." I held up the palms of my hands. "I hope his insurance company isn't one of my company's clients," I said, half-joking.

"We know for a fact that *it is*, and he was told to ask for you by name as his adjuster," Pete said.

"What are you, nuts? I could get in trouble for..." I saw the two grins. I balled up an empty potato chip bag and hurled it at Pete. I knew then that I really was one of them again.

The front door swung open and Martha stepped into the room. She stood staring at us, panting as though out of breath.

"Where's Red?" Johnny asked.

"He, uhh, said he wanted to do some exploring on his own after I pointed out a few areas of interest to him," she answered. She closed the door behind her.

"And he let you come back alone? Don't sound like him. Have you been running?" Pete asked as he stood.

"No, just walking fast to get out of the dark. He said he didn't want me to...to get in any trouble if we were seen together. He'll be right back." Martha pointed to the refrigerator as she sat in a chair across from me. "Can I get a beer?"

Johnny went to the refrigerator, popped the cap off a brown bottle of Rhein-gold, and returned to the table. He handed it to her and she took a long swallow. When she put the half-drained bottle on the table, white foam gushed from the opening. She lit a cigarette with a shaking hand.

"Is something wrong?" I asked.

"No. No, nothing." She took a few hard puffs. "I just, uhh…"

A car door slammed outside and Martha flinched. I was sure that it was Sonny and Lenny. I could hear other cars moving past our building.

Johnny pointed for me to go to the back of the room. I walked to the darker corner, next to the bathroom, and tried to blend into the shadows. Mixed feelings bubbled up from my past, of standing in the corner as a kid being punished and cowering in the dark, having to be protected from someone bigger and stronger than me. I felt like I *was* a child, hoping that I could now face up to Lenny and take away this feeling of inadequacy.

The door opened and Sonny stepped in. I stood rigid and looked past him. Lenny was behind, his full image blocked by Sonny's bulk.

"Sharon!" Sonny stopped just past the doorway and stared at Martha like he had seen a ghost. "What the hell are you…?"

Martha had been sitting sideways on her chair facing the doorway and now slowly stood. She looked startled and stared blankly at Sonny's face. Her sur-prised look turned into a glare and then contempt. "It's you! I remember you from the trial. You were the one that shot my sister. What are you doing out of jail?"

She slowly scanned the room, stopping to concentrate on each of our faces. "Yes, you're older, but I remember some of you now. You guys are the goddamn Vandals. You all helped drive my sister to her nervous breakdowns. Especially you!" She flicked her cigarette at Sonny and then stepped into him with her fists flying. She punched the side of his face and pounded on his chest.

Sonny sidestepped, grabbed her arm, and hurled her backward into Lenny's waiting arms. Lenny wrapped her in a bear hug from behind and tried to calm her. "Easy, honey. Let's talk this over."

Martha drove a spiked heel into Lenny's instep again and again, and he let out a howl. She broke free and spun away, out the open doorway and onto the plat-form. Lenny collapsed into a ball, blocking the doorway. She kicked off her cum-bersome shoes and ran barefoot down the stairs, slapping across the courtyard before we could react.

"Should I get her?" Sonny asked as he tried to sleepwalk over Lenny.

"Too late," Pete said as he raised the window shade. "She's inside the main building. It looks like their party is over, too."

From where I stood, I could see across the courtyard, now that the shade was fully raised and the front door wide open. I saw only three lighted windows on the second floor of the main building. Everything else was dark, and the only music came from the competing tones of the generators. There were three new vehicles parked along the front of the building, which meant there were more of the Renaissance inside. It was eerie that such a loud, tumultuous gathering could become so still within minutes. It felt like an old western movie where the Indian drums had suddenly stopped beating and everyone knew that something was going to happen.

CHAPTER SIXTEEN

Johnny had reached under the dust curtain of the vacant couch and slid out a loaded M16 rifle, two magazines taped together for a quick reload. He dragged a chair to the window, pulled the shade three-quarters down, and began a watch of the area.

Oh, yeah. He said they were ready for trouble.

Lenny sat on the other couch. He had squirmed out of his shoe and sock and was rubbing the bruised blotches surrounding traces of blood where Martha had continually spiked him. He was fortunate that he was wearing heavy-duty work shoes that protected him from even deeper punctures. "Who the fuck was that broad?" he yelled.

"Sharon's sister," Sonny said, still standing in the middle of the floor, staring at the now closed door. "I couldn't believe it when I saw her sitting there. She looked exactly like Sharon did twelve years ago."

"How'd she get in here? I thought we weren't bringing any broads in here," Lenny moaned as he inspected his injury. "We got any Band-Aids?"

"Better. Red brought along an army first aid kit with gauze and tape and other goodies," Pete said. He looked at me and winked as he rummaged through Red's canvas overnight bag next to my resident corner.

"Red was with her," Johnny said from his vigil at the window. "You know how horny military types are. He brought her in to…"

"No, I brought her here," I said before I realized I had. I took a step forward into the light.

Lenny glanced by me as he scanned the room, then came back with a double take so abrupt that I thought I heard his neck snap. His wide-eyed expression was filled with both disbelief and anger.

"You!" Lenny tried to stand, but Pete, with gauze packets, tape roll, and tube of antiseptic ointment in hand, pushed him back onto the couch.

"Let me fix your wound," Pete said.

"Johnny, what did you do here?" Lenny asked.

"Relax," Johnny said. "Just know that he got here on his own with no help from anyone here, but we decided that since he's here, he's staying."

"Who's we?" Lenny shouted. "I didn't get to vote. Sonny didn't, or the Looneys. Who the hell are *we?*"

"Think about the operation," Johnny said. "Let's not break into factions." He turned to Lenny, the M16 pointed at the ceiling. "We have a job to do, and Jim is an extra hand to help finish it. We have no communications with Benny and Kelly for their decision, so let's stay focused, think as one, and use the resources given to us."

I don't know why those few words calmed Lenny or if he just decided that I was impossible to get rid of—for now—but he settled back into the couch and allowed Pete to dress his wound. On second thought, the sight of a loaded rifle in the hands of someone you're arguing with, and who is technically your superior in your organization, probably is a very good backup deterrent.

"Just keep him away from me," Lenny said softly. He stared at me with those hypnotic Rasputin-like wide eyes as though he were willing me to disappear. "I don't want him involved in my part of the operation."

"Fine," Johnny said. "I'll find other things for him to do."

"You know, I can't believe this," Sonny said with his hand outstretched toward me. "Jimmy shows up out of the blue and he tells us he brought Sharon's sister here, and all this after we were supposed to be done with our deal and out of here. What is going on here tonight?"

"Strange coincidences," I said as I moved to the table and sat. "But don't think it's an omen or anything. She just happened to be living here with her brother."

"Her brother?" Sonny sat in a chair across from me. "So the whole damn family is coming after me."

"No, he's a pacifist," I said. "She's all we have to worry about. She'll do anything just to get out of here."

"That's right," Johnny said. "Who knows what stories she's telling them over there?"

"Who cares?" Lenny said. "I brought the samples back from the stash like we agreed. They're not gonna blow this deal over what some wacky broad says. Let's get over there and get this thing moving." He had his sock back on and stood, took one step, and winced. "Son of a bitch." He sat again.

"You may have some ligament damage," Pete said as he bent to Red's bag, putting away the first aid supplies. "It looked like it was starting to swell."

"Rest for a minute," Johnny said. "Didn't they say they'd come here for it? And we gotta wait for Red."

"If you think about it, everything that led to this night started back then in, what was it…1957?" Sonny pondered.

We all nodded, knowing that time in our past very well. We let Sonny fill in the details as we waited for that something from across the way to happen.

"I'm ashamed to admit it, even though you guys already know it's true, but that crazy bitch, Sharon, had my head all screwed up from the minute we started going out. She manipulated me to the point where I made some bad decisions, and she and I were almost entirely responsible for the end of the Vandals—and, more important, for destroying our future business opportunities.

"After I had *accomplished* that, I had nothing left to do but find Sharon and take care of her for her treachery." He paused and stared at the table. "I had a pistol and I found her in an alley. I was gonna do her in when…" He slammed his fist into an open palm. "She conned me again and I weakened. I got rid of the gun and let her get too close and she stabbed me, here…" He lifted his T-shirt and showed a jagged scar alongside his rippled stomach. "Somehow I got hold of the gun again and put one in her.

"Self-defense. It was…self…defense," he trailed off. "But the jury didn't buy it, especially with what the DA added to the pot, like the hit-and-run war and the final rumble with the Sinners that got Blackie killed, the notoriety of the Vandals, and my title as war counselor.

"Sharon pulled through, conned her jury into believing it *was* self-defense on her part, and slinked off into the sunset. I heard she reared her ugly head a few times after that."

"Yeah," Pete said from the other couch. He held out his hand and looked around the room. "Some of us were there the night she came into the bar with a knife."

"I heard about that," Sonny said. "She was still intent on trying to eliminate a gang that no longer existed. After that, she was in and out of the nut house. That's why I was floored when I saw her sister standing here, looking exactly like Sharon. I could've sworn it was her tracking me down again."

"You might not be too far off if her sister is anything like her, and from what I saw, she is," Johnny said.

"Short time as it is, I think I've known grown-up Martha the longest," I said. "And I can tell you that split personalities run in that family."

"Well, anyway, to continue," Sonny said, "I was in the last year of my dozen inside and I got a new cell mate named Victor. He was in for a short stretch for assault and bomb making." Sonny paused. "Sorry," he said to Pete and Johnny.

They nodded and motioned for him to continue.

"Victor called himself a revolutionary and was part of a group named Renaissance. He told me that his group was always in the market for guns. I told him I knew people who could get them, as long as the price was right. This was my chance for redemption for what I had done back in fifty-seven." Sonny's face beamed with fulfillment. "I had someone contact Kelly for me and Victor contacted his people and we quietly—while still in the can—put together a big ticket deal. Maybe it wouldn't amount to what we lost in those years our guys weren't earning, but it was a start on my road back.

"Victor and me both got out of the joint within a few weeks of each other and started to work out some details. Then Victor hits me with this request for chemical weapons. Do we know anyone who can get us a bunch of chemical gas canisters with military markings? His boss will squelch the deal unless we can get chemicals.

"I'm looking bad to Kelly and Benny, who have already laid out some seed money, when I'm supposed to be working my way back into their good graces..."

"That's when Red got into the picture," Johnny said. "By the way, he's been out quite a while. He usually doesn't take this long to scout something."

"If he can find his way through a jungle in Vietnam, he can find his way back here," Pete said.

"Yeah, I guess so," Johnny said. "Well, anyway, Red enters to save the day."

"That's for damn sure," Sonny said. "And to save my bacon."

"There's a lot of this that's top secret and that Red couldn't talk about," Johnny said, turning back to the window. "But this is what I know from my part in it and what Red told me. He's currently assigned to military intelligence, and MI has its own files on radical groups, separate from the FBI. While he was home on leave and visiting the club, Kelly approached him about how chemical weapons are stored and disposed and whatever he could tell him. Kelly knew Red would never set up a theft of any military equipment. He was only trying to get a handle on how hard it was to get hold of the stuff.

"As it turned out, the name Renaissance was mentioned, and it rang a bell with Red from some files he had been reviewing. To make the story short, he approached his colonel, who put it to a higher authority, got permission to set up an operation, and supplied Red with what they thought he would need.

"Kelly put his deal together. And with the gas cylinders thrown in, a lot more bucks were renegotiated. Part of the deal with the army was for Red to come along to gather intel on these monkeys. He was able to convince his CO that he had to work alone, that it would spook his contacts to have strangers involved. That's why we decided to use you, Jimmy, instead of a member of Red's unit to pick up the stuff. We figured to keep it in the family and give you a shot at being involved, but not involved, so to speak. Of course, that was then, before you showed up here and..." Johnny turned and looked at Lenny, then back to the window.

"Anyway, all the preparations were made months ago, waiting for word from Renaissance for a definite delivery date. Red even got the rifles as a bonus so Kelly didn't have to deal with other contacts who were going to wholesale guns to him at a big piece of his profit."

I was glad to be hearing these explanations. I was relieved to know Red wasn't some kind of rogue soldier selling out his country. But I wished we didn't have to be involved with that damn sarin. It bothered me to know that the army would take a chance on letting that junk be used as a bargaining chip.

"So, one minute everything is on hold," Johnny said. "And then, bang, the ball drops. They need everything now, before this weekend. We get our end rolling, everyone gears up, and..." Johnny sighed. "Well, then this unfortunate development..."

"Why Johnny and I are here," Pete filled in.

"Hey, something's happening," Johnny said, bringing the M16 to his shoulder and pointing it along the window.

We all rushed to the window, except for Lenny, who hobbled, using Sonny for support. I squeezed between Sonny and Pete, and we hunched behind Johnny.

The scene outside the factory looked like what it would have in the building's productive era. People flowed out the wide-open double doorway in the main building, as though the whistle had blown at the end of the workday. Some of the Renaissance and their ladies hopped on the Harleys in front or piled into the vans and pickups. Most of the Renaissance soldiers stayed on foot and crossed to the rear building, resembling a swarm of bees entering their hive through several doors. The wrought-iron gates were open, and a group of guards stood near them.

After the roar of engines had died and bluish exhaust smoke had clouded the lights and those leaving the yard had left, two of the members, in their customary vest uniforms, crossed toward us. One of them was pushing a hand truck, and the other had a briefcase.

"The shorter guy with the long hair is Victor," Sonny said. "They must be coming for the stuff. I'll go talk to him."

"No, you both do," Johnny said. "Lenny, lean at the door so they don't know you're hurt and do your talking from there. I'll cover from here, and the rest of you go out on the platform for support."

Sonny helped Lenny to the door, opened it, and stepped out. Johnny motioned for Pete and me to follow. I moved to the end of the platform near the closed corrugated steel cargo door that opened into the large area behind the dorm room.

"How's it going, my man?" Sonny asked Victor as he moved down the stairs.

"Cool," Victor said as they slapped skin and then shook. "This is Jerome." Victor's bald, overweight companion leaning on the hand truck nodded. "Who gets the loot?"

Sonny took the briefcase and walked it up to Lenny, who opened it. From where I stood on the platform, I could see a layer of banded twenty-dollar bills across the bottom of the case. Lenny leaned against the doorjamb and flipped through the packs of bills.

He nodded an OK and closed the case.

Sonny opened the deck lid of the Buick, and he and Jerome lifted a yellow cylinder of sarin from a wooden, padded, makeshift securing device built into the trunk compartment. They carefully placed it on the hand truck, and Jerome wrapped a length of chain several times around the cylinder and secured it with a lock.

Sonny lifted an unloaded AR15 from the trunk compartment and handed it to Victor.

"No ammo?" Victor asked.

"You get the ammo when you get the full load of weapons," Lenny said as he slung the briefcase to his side. "This is just to show your boss what our merchandise looks like."

"OK." Victor shook Sonny's hand again and Jerome nodded. "All of the bread is here now," Victor said. "So you can bring everything in and we'll get together over at the headquarters building."

"Headquarters building?" Sonny asked.

"Yeah." Victor pointed at the main building across the yard. "Park the army trucks in front, and I'll be waiting for you at the doors to show you the way up to see the Leader."

"What's that building back there?" I asked, pointing to where the dispersing mob had retreated.

"That's our barracks. They're all going to catch a couple hours of Z's before we head out."

"Head out?" Sonny asked.

"Maybe you'll find out later. That's up to the Leader," Victor said. "Give us about an hour. The guards know what kind of vehicles you'll be bringing in, and they're instructed to let you pass. OK?"

Lenny nodded. "See you in an hour," he said.

Jerome wheeled the sarin across the yard and Victor toted the AR15. The wheels of the hand truck squeaked as they bounced along the cobblestones. When the two reached the entrance of their headquarters building, Victor slung the rifle over his shoulder and lifted the bottom of the dolly over the threshold. Then they disappeared behind the closed door.

CHAPTER SEVENTEEN

We had passed two reinforced guard posts, about a mile apart, in our trip past the bald mountain and down the factory road toward the outside world. The posts had been on either side of the road, and each contained one vehicle with an attached spotlight to illuminate their area, along with a few motorcycles, which they would probably use for a chase, if necessary, and about a half dozen Renaissance soldiers. Security had been beefed up in anticipation of whatever was about to take place. We were told that a final doomsday post, past where we were heading and just before a highway, had been put in place weeks ago and was ordered to let no one through, not even the Leader, until after a specified secret time. Shoot to kill without discretion were their orders.

Johnny was driving the Chevy, Pete at shotgun position with a sawed-off pump shotgun in his lap, and me in the backseat. Johnny had convinced Lenny to rest his foot and was going to leave me with him but thought better, and after some whispered last-minute strategy between them, he asked Sonny to stay and help guard our area and wait for Red. We had left Sonny with the M16 at the window and Lenny counting the down payment money, holding every third or fourth bill up to the light to be sure they weren't counterfeit.

We were three miles past the last guard post when Johnny slowed the Chevy and hunched forward to strain his eyes through the night and into the forest.

"There it is," Pete said. He pointed ahead of us and into the trees.

Johnny angled the car toward the forest so the headlamps lit the trees and stopped. Pete jumped out and moved clumps of dried brush that had been strung together and tied to a tree on either side of a hidden trail. Johnny pulled the

Chevy onto the trail, stopped, and waited for Pete to reset the concealment bushes and get back into the car.

"This is an old logging camp trail," Johnny explained. "We're pretty sure that no one knows about it, and it's miles away from where the Renaissance patrol their perimeter." He turned off the headlights. "We'll wait for a couple of minutes to be sure no one was following us."

"How'd you come across it?" I asked.

"As soon as we found out where we were going, we contacted the local county records department, told them we were from a land development company, and got access to maps of the area." Johnny turned on the lights again and started the Chevy forward. "Sonny and Red made a dry run a few days ago and secretly scouted the terrain. These trails and the camp showed up on an old archive chart, and luckily, most of the trail stayed intact and free of overgrowth. Until here."

The trail had been rough and only as wide as the Chevy, but now it narrowed to the size of a footpath.

"This is where we get out and walk," Pete announced. He took the shotgun with him when he left the car. "Jimmy, grab that dry cell spotlight on the floor back there."

Johnny turned out the headlights and shut off the ignition. I snapped on the dry cell and handed it to Johnny after I stepped out of the car. The three of us started up the path.

We walked along the corridor through the trees for about thirty yards until we reached a clearing, and there it was, like a giant resting dinosaur. The tractor-trailer stretched out along the entire length of one side of the square-acre lot. It had suffered more damage since I'd last seen it, was missing chunks of the fiberglass cab and the front bumper was bent and jammed back into the radiator. The front panel and part of the roof of the trailer were buckled. I hoped that Johnny and Pete *were* only kidding about the fraudulent insurance claim and their request for my involvement.

The only other thing on the lot was a bare cinder block and concrete foundation in the far corner, housing just a brick fireplace with a collapsed chimney. Johnny shone the light around the lot and then turned it off for a few seconds before turning it on again. Another light flashed on and off and on again from the cab of the tractor.

"Who's there?" Pat Looney called out from behind the light. He shone it directly at us and we were momentarily blinded.

"Johnny and Pete," Johnny yelled, his hand up to block out the glare.

The light went out and we approached the tractor. The driver's door swung open and Pat slid out, ignored the cab sidestep, and dropped straight to the ground.

"Anything happening yet?" Pat asked. Then he saw me. "Who is...? That's not..."

"Yeah, it's me," I said.

"Where's your brother?" Johnny asked before Pat could put together a sentence.

"Right here," a voice said from behind us.

We turned and found a grinning Mike Looney with an M16 pointed into the air. "We could hear you mugs coming a mile away," he said. "What's up? It's too early to be relieved."

"It's on," Johnny said. "We came to move the stuff up to the compound."

"Yeah!" the brothers shouted in unison. Then Mike asked, "So what's with Jimmy boy, here?"

Johnny gave a brief explanation of what had happened, emphasizing that I was part of the team. The Looneys shrugged in agreement and walked away to prepare for the move. It would be very rare if the Looneys questioned any decision by a superior. They were the consummate subordinates. Give them a task, point them in the right direction, and they were happy. Just make sure you got out of their way.

Johnny had me walk to the rear of the lot with him, and I looked into the open trailer. At first I thought the darkness was playing tricks with my eyes, but then Johnny shone the light into the interior and I saw that the trailer was empty. Then he shone the light into the trees behind us. Pat was folding back the end of a camouflage net that was draped over one of the M37s. The truck was surrounded by a grove of trees, and with the netting in place and its own camouflage paint scheme, it appeared to be part of the landscape. Johnny shone the light across the lot, past the remnant foundation, and highlighted Mike and Pete pulling the netting off the other M37.

Both of the trucks were started and revving up within a few minutes.

"They brought the trailer in by that wider trail back there." Johnny pointed the light at an opening in the rear of the lot. There were deep tire ruts leading back through the trees. "We unloaded the trucks and hid them just in case someone happened onto the camp. As you can see, they're invisible in the dark."

"So, how are we dividing up into the vehicles?" I asked.

"The Looneys will be driving the trucks, and Pete and I will each ride security."

"And I'll drive the Chevy?"

"Yes. You'll bring up the rear," Johnny said. "I'll guide you back off the trail. When we reach the main road, back down a little to give the trucks room to swing out. Then follow us. When we get inside the gate, park at our platform and go in and get Lenny and Sonny—and I guess Red will be back—and bring them over to finalize the deal. One of them will drive the Buick over. Keep the engine running, and we'll be back out to the cars shortly."

"Will do."

"I'm glad you decided to listen to reason and knock off your search to be a macho guy."

"Oh, I realized at some point tonight that I had proven myself just by getting here. I came here to help you, and I'm here helping you. Now I just have to finish the job so I never have to doubt that inner strength again."

"You know you never had to prove anything to me, or anyone else, for that matter," Johnny said. "I still remember when we were kids and we talked things over, helped get one another through the rough spots, like when the people I lived with gave me a bad time or kicked me out into the cold. Or when your parents were too busy to listen, too busy working at menial jobs to scrape together enough money just to live on so they had no spare time for you. I was out on the streets as the orphan and you were the latchkey kid. We understood what it was like to have no one to confide in, to listen to what was inside us. We helped each other. That's when you proved yourself, because it's inside where the courage is, not playing a tough guy."

"That was a long time ago," I said. "We grew up and made different lives for ourselves, but I'm glad you can still remember. I know I only had to prove things to myself, but I appreciate you telling me that."

Johnny's face was shadowy in the artificial glow of the spotlight, but I could see in his eyes that we *were* kids again and he had something more to tell me. "You ever killed anyone?"

Me? "No! You know I haven't. But why?"

"You know what? Neither have I. That's right, my position behind Benny and Kelly was gained by knowing how to make numbers work, not by strong-arming or killing. I think you may have known that deep down because you do know me inside."

"Yeah, no matter how much I thought otherwise on the surface, I did believe that and I'm glad to know it's true."

"That's why I'll always be in that same position, behind Benny and Kelly," Johnny continued. "I know my limitations, and I think it's something you probably learned about yourself tonight. I'm not here to kill for the company's money, if need be, like Lenny and the Looneys. I'm here, along with Pete, for revenge. Like you suspected, we're sure that the guy who killed Madge is here. This is something I've never done before but need to do now. Both Pete and I will do it. You might think, well, why couldn't we have Lenny or one of the other guys take care of the bastard for us and save us a trip?"

"No. I think if I were in Pete's or your spot, I would want to be the one that took care of my own closure." *That is, if I had the guts to actually kill someone. Yeah, I guess that part is something I really don't want to know.*

"Exactly. The thing is, I don't think that those people are gonna let us just walk in there and kill one of theirs without answering back."

I shook my head, and the realism rattled around inside. This was the "and then you do what you have to do" part of Johnny's message. I don't know why I had been so naïve not thinking—especially with all the guns being waved around—that this night would end in gunfire. Maybe I thought that they would commit poetic justice and blow up the Renaissance by a remote control bomb after we left with the money, or shoot some of them to settle the score while we were driving away. Wishful thinking.

"So keep that engine running and be ready to goose it. We'll be depending on you."

"You sure I can't be with you when…"

"No. Your job is just as important. You'll be helping every one of us by your actions."

I smiled and nodded. I was satisfied with my role and, most of all, I was satisfied with myself. I didn't need to know about that deep, dark part of myself anymore. Maybe I'm really a pacifist like Clarence and his people. Maybe that's what I learned on this trip. Like Johnny said, I now know my limitations. Just like the Looneys, I would do as told. And whatever had bothered me about selling the sarin and AR15s to the Renaissance was temporarily behind me. I would have to live with that later.

"Come on." Johnny turned and started back toward the center of the lot where the Looneys had maneuvered the M37s behind one another, facing the footpath. Their headlights illuminated the path so well that I could make out a reflection off the bumper of the Chevy in the distance.

I followed Johnny past the trucks, waved to Pete and the Looneys, and started down the path. When we reached the Chevy, we stopped.

"Thanks, Johnny," I said as I slid into the driver's seat and started the engine. "And good luck."

"You, too, buddy. See you on the way home."

Johnny walked a few yards down the path and I kept the spot on him. He waved for me to come back. I shifted into reverse and slowly backed down the trail. Just before I reached the road, I heard a roar and a crashing sound like the forest was being decimated by a giant chainsaw. I looked forward and saw the lead M37 come smashing through the saplings and foliage at the head of the trail like a bowling ball battering a wedge of pins.

I swung the Chevy past Johnny, who had cleared away the layer of brush, and continued backing down the road until I was clear of the trail. The trucks reached the road, Johnny jumped into the front one, and they headed back toward the factory. I could only hope that whatever was about to happen went according to plan and that we all got out of there safely. I would do my best in my new role to help make that happen.

CHAPTER EIGHTEEN

The iron gates closed behind me and I wondered if the front end of the Chevy would be strong enough to crash them open when the time came. I nosed the Chevy to the platform support next to the Buick. I watched in the rear view mirror as the two M37s parked at the headquarters building. No one exited the trucks. I was waiting for something to happen, and after a couple of minutes I realized that maybe I was the one that everyone was waiting on. I guessed I'd better check inside with the others like Johnny had instructed. There was light behind the window shade but no movement.

I climbed the stairs and opened the unlocked door. I stepped inside and was looking into the muzzle of the M16. For some strange reason, the opening seemed larger than it was, and I could clearly see the rifling along the inside of the barrel. And it was in the hands of Lenny. He sat on the couch facing the door, a cigarette dangling from his lips and his swollen shoeless foot propped on one of the chairs.

"Get in here and close the door," Lenny ordered.

I thought about spinning out the door and off the platform, but my better judgment calculated that I couldn't compete with the speed of a bullet. It's funny how many silly or trivial things can run through a person's mind at a time like this. I closed the door and looked around the room. Lenny and I were alone.

My heart began to pound to the point where I could feel the vibration in my chest. It was finally over—or it would be in another moment or two. What would Lenny say to Johnny and the others? He thought it was a Renaissance guy breaking in? He fired without thinking? Gee, too bad. If only I had known it was Jimmy. *If I had known it was Jimmy, I'd have fired a few more rounds into him.*

"Where's Sonny?" was all I could think of saying, like Sonny would come out of the bathroom and plead my case and save me.

"He went to look for Red," Lenny said. "Sit!"

I dropped into the closest chair, feeling like a puppy responding to a command. *What was he going to do, mentally torture me before he pulled the trigger?*

"Red still is missing?"

"Yeah." He lowered the rifle, shifted his shoeless foot, and grimaced. The swelling and bandages made the arch of his foot look like a baseball had been stuffed under his sock. He dragged on his cigarette and placed it in a table ashtray. "Did you really bust your ass to get here to help us?"

"Yes." I wasn't going to embellish on my trip. It might sound like pandering—or worse, groveling.

"And you knew I was here?"

"I tried my best to avoid you but, yeah, I was sure this moment would eventually happen."

"You got balls I never knew you had. I respect that. But what's your angle?"

"Angle?"

"Everyone of us is here for a reason. I'm here to make sure we get our bread, the Looneys are here to make a few bucks out of the deal, Sonny to atone for his past sins, Red to spy, and Pete and Johnny for revenge. Where do you fit in?"

"You're a very perceptive guy." I paused to let the compliment set in. "I'm here to do whatever I can."

"Stop the shit. Nobody does what you did just to be Santa's helper. You wanna look good to Johnny and Pete and maybe Kelly and Benny, too. Maybe all this changed you. Maybe you decided you *were* a sucker and now you want a better paying job with us?"

"None of the above. What I came here to accomplish, I'll finish when we all drive through those gates for the last time."

"Look." Lenny held up his hand. "I don't need any psycho mumbo-jumbo to know that once we get out of here, things will be better all around. So whatever your reason, the name of the game is to get the hell out of here. We can't wait for those guys anymore. They'll have to bring the Buick over with them when they catch up. Come on, help me out to the Chevy and we'll finish this thing."

Lenny leaned the butt of the M16 on the floor for support and stood. He crushed out the cigarette in the ashtray. I put my arm around him and tried to match his gait as we moved to the door.

"Then…" *I had to ask, to know if…*"What you said earlier, back at the warehouse toilet, is off? I don't have to go into hiding?"

"Are you kidding? When I come home with the payoff, I'll be back in good standing, business-wise. But what you did to me, I'll never live down."

"But you said…" I stopped when we reached the door and took a breath. "You said things would be better all around. That doesn't make things better for me."

"You won't be dead. That's better."

"But that means I won't be able to visit the club anymore, or see any of my friends."

"That's right." Lenny slung the rifle strap over his shoulder and opened the door. "You'll get over it."

"And what if I happen to show up?" We stepped through the doorway onto the platform. "What happens?"

"Then we go back to original option number two."

Maybe I would try to convince him otherwise later, when we were out of here, or ask him if I could publicly apologize to him in front of Kelly and Benny, or anything else that would save his face and return me to my status quo. It was funny that I wouldn't grovel for my life, but I would do it for my social standing. He was right about one thing, we had to first think about getting out of here before anything else, but it was good to know that at least I could now talk to him. He didn't seem as crazy as his reputation anymore, and, strangely, I now resigned myself to trust in him.

I helped him down the stairs and into the passenger seat of the Chevy. I got behind the wheel, and we were across the yard and parked next to the M37s in two minutes. Lenny swung open his door.

"Where the hell are they?" Lenny asked above the noise of the M37 engines. The Looneys waved to us from behind the steering wheels. "Where are Johnny and Pete?" he shouted louder to Mike in the closest truck.

"They met some guy at the door and went up," Mike answered.

"Sonny?"

"No, one of the guys from here. A long-haired guy that said he was Sonny's friend. They told us to tell you to wait here for them and for us to keep the engines running and wait for their signal before we leave the trucks."

"Something's wrong. I gotta get up there," Lenny said as he grasped the open door and pulled himself to his feet. "Help me up the stairs," he yelled to me as he bent his head back into the car.

"I'm not supposed to leave the Chevy. I…"

"The plan's changed. They weren't supposed to go up alone. They may be in trouble." Lenny slung the M16 over his shoulder again. "Help me up the stairs."

I left the engine running and slid out my door. Johnny wasn't going to like this, but what could I do? Lenny had a rifle and he was ordering me to do something. *What could I do?* I had to get him up the stairs, up to where they were. "Coming, mother."

"Don't leave those trucks or let anyone try to take them from you without the passwords," Lenny reminded the Looneys.

Mike displayed the barrel of his M16. "No problem."

We stepped to the entrance doors and I yanked one of the heavy portals open. There were two steep staircases to the sides of the small, dimly lit, empty vestibule. Directly in front of us was a door with broken upper glass panes covered over with corrugated cardboard. The staircases were mounted against a blank plaster wall that rose twenty feet from the top of the center door to the next floor with a landing break about halfway. There were muffled voices coming from the top of the right set of stairs, so we started up that incline. I had Lenny use the banister, and I supported his other side as he hopped a step at a time on his uninjured foot. We were two steps from the top when a pair of large oak pocket doors with frosted glass inserts slid open and two Renaissance troops carrying AK47s stepped into the entrance hall.

"We'll take that weapon," one of them said, pointing at Lenny. He had a reddish blond beard and a black bandana around his head. The other guy was baldheaded Jerome.

I felt Lenny twist his body in an attempt to hastily bring the M16 to use, but our arms got tangled and he almost slipped and fell. He saw both the AK47s pointed at us and decided to hand over his weapon. We were then ordered through the doorway.

CHAPTER NINETEEN

Lenny and I stepped into a well-lit room the size of a small school auditorium, and I coughed from the stale odor of marijuana hanging heavy in the air. The room was furnished with three lines of trash-strewn gray wooden tables and matching benches and resembled a prison dining hall just after a riot. The tables were empty of people. In front of us, facing the main table area, was a long formal dining room table that was old but not quite antique and was similar to the one in our dorm room. There were five people—Renaissance people—sitting behind the table on matched padded chairs. They were staring at us. Two flags hung on the wall behind them, a United States flag with a peace sign replacing the stars in the field of blue and a North Vietnam flag. I cringed but swallowed my pride and tried to avoid looking at them. Lenny and I were given a quick cursory frisk. The guards leaned the M16 next to Pete's sawed-off shotgun in a corner against the far wall, acknowledged that we were clean, and then moved back outside the room and closed the doors.

Johnny, Pete, and Sonny sat in front of the five on white wooden chairs that looked like they came from a kitchen set of a fifties television program. The way they sat, the three of them looked like they were either being granted an audience or being tried for some crime. Victor and two others in Renaissance gear stood at the other side of the VIP table where a bank of eight-foot-high windows over-looking the courtyard began and ran for most of the length of the room.

"Welcome. Join your friends." He sat behind the head table, and his centered chair was high-backed with ornate carvings along the top. He was mid-twenties in age and, although sitting, appeared to be the shortest of the group. He wore a trimmed goatee, and with his premature loss of hair resembled—purposely or not—Lenin. "I am the *Leader* of the Renaissance."

"What kind of crap you pulling here, Mr. Leader?" Lenny asked. "Don't think you're dealing with some kind of street punks who you can rip off."

"Not at all. Not at all," the Leader said with his hand raised and fluttering in a welcoming gesture. "You must be Lenny, the negotiator."

"What's going on, Johnny?" Lenny asked.

Johnny slid the last available kitchen chair over to Lenny, and the legs scraped loudly against the worn linoleum floor. Johnny looked at me knowingly, and I was sure he was pissed at me for conniving my way up here. "Sonny's pal, Victor, helped lure us up here," he said to Lenny.

Lenny looked at Sonny, then Victor. Victor turned away to look out the window. Lenny sat, and I moved back even with the wall.

Sonny shrugged. "He told me that you guys were already here and wanted to see me," he said. "Then he told Johnny and Pete that I was hurt and needed their help. He showed them my jacket to prove I was here." He looked at Victor, who still had his back turned, looking out the window. "I wouldn't trust any of these scumbags."

I folded my arms and leaned against the wall a few feet from the doorway. *Talk about being connived.* Johnny's got no reason to chastise me.

I took a minute in the lull after Sonny's unanswered insult to study the VIP table. The four members other than the Leader were all in their denim or leather vests, and each wore a different-colored beret, probably to show their rank or organizational designation. The Leader was the only one without a hat, and he wore a unique solid red vest with two brass stars pinned over his heart. I scanned all their faces again and found that Snark wasn't there. I certainly would have thought he was a member of the leadership corps the way he had exercised command in town.

"Just the two big Irish guys left?" the Leader asked Victor.

Victor nodded.

"OK, go get…"

"I wouldn't do that, if I were you, Mr. Leader," Lenny said. "Not unless you want your boy dead, and whoever goes after him in the same shape. Their orders are to not leave those trucks without all of us being present and a series of passwords given. Believe me that they follow orders to the death if necessary. They're not known as the Looney brothers for nothing."

"Well…" The Leader stared at the table as though evaluating the situation. "It looks like we have a standoff, doesn't it? But, you know, I have almost my full contingency of troops now. I can order a mass attack that would overwhelm those two, and even if I lost several people, I'd still have more than enough to complete my mission."

"And that would be just about the time that both trucks blew sky high from the rigged charges activated by the drivers' dead man switches. Then what would you have? Nothing but a big hole where this place used to stand and a big cloud of poison gas in the air."

"Ah, touché," the Leader said. "We're back to our standoff again, providing what you say is true."

"You willing to risk everything to find out? Do you think we'd walk in here unprotected like a bunch of yokels?"

The Leader stared at Lenny, trying to read his poker face for almost a minute, then turned to one of the men standing with Victor and beckoned with his finger. The soldier walked behind the table and leaned the side of his head next to the Leader. There were a few whispers, and the man nodded and then returned to his position at the window.

"OK, now, what the hell is your problem?" Lenny asked. "We have the merchandise and you have the money—so you say. Let's make the exchange as agreed and part our ways."

"You don't want to know what is going to take place, what all those items you delivered are going to be used for?"

"Why would we want to know?" Lenny asked. "I just want our money—and that little piece of information we asked for. You can do whatever you want with those items once you paid for them."

"Please, indulge me," the Leader huffed. "I was about to brief my staff with the final details of our plan before you all dropped in. It may affect your future, you know."

Lenny looked around the room at each of us. "If it'll get us the money and our final request, fine. Except, I want to see the cash to know you got it, I want someone posted at the window to make sure none of your people are trying to pull something outside, I want the information we asked for, and I want our weapons back."

"My, but you drive a hard bargain. No weapons until you leave this complex. Wouldn't want anyone getting hurt. We would like to do business again after our victory and wish to complete our bargain, which is why we'll pass on that information that you asked for a little later. By the way, I should reduce the price we agreed upon." The Leader had one of his subordinates lift a suitcase from under the table and place it on top. "You're walking around with M16s and all you can find for us is obsolete AR15s?" He smiled. "Actually we needed the extra rifles for the shock troops. Our elite members are armed with the superior AK47, a product of the Soviet worker."

He opened the valise. It was packed with rows of bills bound with paper wrappers, neat and sharp like laundered green print shirts packed for a trip. "One and a half million dollars, less the ten thousand given to you earlier."

Lenny stood, and Johnny helped him to the table. They both counted the stacks and scrutinized some of the bills individually. I was sure they were checking to be sure that there weren't plain strips of paper or obvious counterfeits substituted under the top bills and that the serial numbers weren't consecutive.

"Sorry about your injury, Lenny," the Leader said.

Lenny looked up from his task. "If I see that bitch again who did it, she'll be sorry."

"Oh, I'm sure she only did it in panic, from what I'm told," the Leader said. "We'll talk about her later, also."

"Oh?" Lenny dismissed the subject with a wave of his hand. "OK with the bread. Everything looks good. Jimmy, you wanna check out the window?" Lenny said as he and Johnny returned to their kitchen chairs. "Keep an eye down below and be sure to tell us if anyone comes anywhere near those trucks."

"M…Me?" I hesitated for a moment, looked at Johnny, who gave me a slight nod of approval, and then started across the front of the desk. I stopped and looked down at the rows of hundred dollar bills in the valise. I was sure it would be the only time in my life that I ever saw a million plus dollars in one place. The Leader slammed the lid of the suitcase closed and stared at me with a slight curl in his lip like I was a peasant or a buck private in his army. Then I knew why he had our guys sitting on those ridiculous chairs, to ridicule them and make them seem inferior to him. All except me to this point, but now I was personally disparaged.

A door opened somewhere past us down a sparingly lit long corridor, and heels clicked on the hard linoleum floor. A Renaissance soldier emerged from the corridor archway and crossed in front of me. He leaned down to the Leader to deliver a private message. I slowed my pace and strained my hearing capabilities but could only make out a few words before I passed the table and reached the first window. The soldier was apparently reporting about something taking place in a chamber. When he was done, the Leader whispered to him and the courier returned down the passageway.

Victor and his two companions moved back to the second window to give me a perch at the first. I looked down into the courtyard and saw only the two M37s and the Chevy, exhaust smoke still flowing from their tailpipes. I wondered if I should have left the Chevy running and if it had enough gas. The iron entrance gates were closed, and I couldn't see any guards.

"Everything's quiet," I said.

"Now, Mr. Leader, what's so important for us to hear?" Lenny asked.

CHAPTER TWENTY

"At exactly noon tomorrow...," the Leader said, looking at his watch. "Or should I say today, Sunday, the vehicle with the sarin GB cylinders will be parked in the middle of a pasture in Bethel, New York. It will be slightly disguised with an amateur paint job but not disguised too much, so that a future investigation will reveal it and the cylinders to be owned by the U.S. Army. The caps of the cylinders will be molded with just enough C4 explosives needed for the task, all connected by wiring and electronic receivers. Once a signal is sent to those receivers, the caps will blow along with the canvas covering and enough sarin will be released to kill and sicken thousands of people.

"So you say, so what, it's in the middle of a pasture. You'll kill some cows or horses?" The Leader smiled, obviously enjoying his long-drawn-out commentary, thinking it was creating drama. "But, no. That pasture is now filled with those thousands of people. There's a music festival that started this last Friday and is scheduled to end tonight. It's called Woodstock, and it has amassed crowds beyond what anyone could ever imagine. I can't believe the luck. When I planned this, I thought there would be only a few thousand attendees. Now with tens of thousands, it will be much more effective. People are camped in the fields, crammed together where they can easily be overcome by the sarin before it eventually dissipates. The roads are jammed with vehicles. Emergency vehicles will have great difficulty getting to the affected area. The U.S. Army will be responsible for the worst massacre of civilians in all history, not to mention some of those civilians being celebrity musicians, loved and cherished by many. And those civilians, famous and not, will be lovers of peace who only wanted to gather together to celebrate that peace and that love, only to be murdered by our treacherous government."

Everyone seated on the kitchen chairs stared with silent, tightly pressed lips or open dumbfounded mouths. For some strange reason, I could only think of the first words uttered when the telegraph or telephone or something like that was invented. *What has God wrought?* How could He have created this sick bastard? And we're contributing to this insanity? I looked at Johnny, and he gave the slightest shake of his head. *Let it go,* he was saying. Let the crackpot finish his spiel. They were waiting for him to finish so we could thank him and be on our way, maybe drop a dime once we hit some kind of civilization and stop this madness. And there was something familiar about the name, Woodstock. I had heard it before.

"But you'll be killing people who do support some of your goals," Pete said, being the first to come out of the trance that the Leader had spun. "Why would you…?"

"In wars and revolutions, some must die to further the cause. They will be martyred with statues and the place of their deaths will be preserved as hallowed ground."

"So, you say you'd order the death of *anyone*—anyone who stood in your way?" Pete asked as he slowly rose from his chair.

Johnny grabbed Pete's arm and pulled him back to his seat. "Why do you think that the army will be suspected?" Johnny asked. "There will be calmer heads who'll know that anyone could've planted that truck there other than the army."

"Well, that's where someone you know will help convince everyone," the Leader said.

"Who?" Lenny asked.

"Your redheaded friend, the army spy who came with you."

"Red? What…"

"I told you I'd discuss Martha at a later time." The Leader interlaced his fingers in front of him and leaned back into his chair. "Well, she helped get him to walk into our trap. She'll be rewarded with her freedom, which she's wanted for so long. Actually, she did it for nothing." He laughed with almost a feminine titter. "We were going to pull out of here tonight and only leave a small garrison to guard our marijuana fields. She could have left at any time she wanted after that."

"What the hell you want Red for?" Lenny asked. "He came here with us, he leaves with us."

"Sorry. That's something you can't negotiate. I've kept you here, telling you my plans, to give us time to prepare him. He's probably dead by now, so it would be a moot point."

"Dead?" A few of us said it in a chorus.

"We know he's military intelligence, or is that an oxymoron?" He giggled this time. "He was seen at an airport with his MI insignia on his uniform." He pointed the two forefingers of his still interlocked hands at Lenny and the others. "Accompanied by three of you."

I remembered the hippies at LaGuardia. They're part of the Renaissance?

"We have our own spy network, as well. It takes one to…Well, you get the idea. But I'm straying from the plan. Your MI pal has been locked in an airtight chamber, conveniently left intact from the previous owners of this site, and has been subjected to the contents of the cylinder of sarin that you gave us as a sample. Last word I got is that he's dead and my second in command is waiting for whatever residual gas there is to escape harmlessly through some outside vents so he can have the body removed."

"You son of a bitch." Pete tried to stand again but was restrained by Johnny.

"Please, don't mourn for someone like that. We don't blame you for bringing him here. We're sure that he used his past friendship as a means to infiltrate your ranks just so he could wangle his way here. Just forget about him. His body will be placed in the vehicle with the sarin, and it will appear that he was one of those who released the gas but didn't have time to escape. His foot will be wedged in or under something as though he became trapped as the gas was released. There will be incriminating equipment and documents on his person, and he will be traced back to some covert operation that, in fact, supplied this very sarin. That will be most convincing. Don't you think?"

No one answered. Pete's head was bowed. I looked out the window and saw that everything below was still as we had left it. I tried to think of where it was I had heard about Woodstock.

"OK, so you got one of ours," Lenny said. He raised his hand when he saw the Leader about to further vilify Red. "We'll give you that in exchange for the one we want. Then we'll take our money and leave."

"Fair enough. It was part of our agreement. We don't want to let some fool who screwed up and missed his target be protected. I don't want to damage the relationship we can have between your organization and ours. After all, business must continue after the revolution, and your people know how to handle certain businesses."

Yes, Woodstock. I didn't hear it. I read it. I reached into my jacket's upper pocket and pulled out the paper Gwen had written the directions on. The flip side was an advertisement for the Woodstock Festival. My God. That's where Gwen was going to be. And she would be there on Sunday. Today. She'll be there when they discharge the sarin. "Johnny, no, you can't let them do it. Gwen…Gwen is going to be at Woodstock!"

I started forward, holding the paper in front of me and shaking it, and was immediately grabbed by the two Renaissance behind me. "You can't put that stuff in their hands," I shouted.

"What is this?" the Leader asked, annoyed.

"Never mind about him," Lenny said. "We'll calm him down." He limped forward and gripped the suitcase handle. "Have the bomber outside in five minutes and we'll release the trucks to you."

"Lenny! Johnny!" I shouted. "How can you…"

"You can bring the person with you right now," the Leader said as he stood. "It's your old pal, Victor." He pointed behind me and nodded to the pair who held me. "He set off the bomb in your associate's catering hall."

The two Renaissance released their hold on my arms and turned to a wide-eyed Victor. They grabbed him and pinned his arms behind his back.

"Wait. You can't tell them that. I…I've always been loyal." Victor struggled against the strength of his larger captors. "Why are you doing this to me? You're not going to pin this on me entirely. I was told to plant that bomb. He ordered me." He stretched his neck forward to point his head at the Leader. "He said your people in that part of the city were muscling into our marijuana sales. He knew what he was doing. It had nothing to do with politics or the revolution. He knew it was the right target. It just detonated too soon."

All heads turned to the Leader as everyone on both sides of the table now rose to their feet.

"He's obviously rambling and lying through his teeth. He's just trying to save his own skin," the Leader said. "But luckily no one of any significance was killed by his mistake. None of your associates were harmed. Only some inconsequential old woman who worked there…"

Pete reached inside the front of his pants like he was trying to scratch his crotch. His face was flushed and his eyes were glazed. A small Beretta pistol whipped out from his pants and swung toward the Leader. The shots made low popping sounds, and the top half of the Leader's right ear disappeared as the side of his head burst open in a spurt of red. The Leader jerked into his chair and tipped backward, and one of his officers slumped over him just as two more officers leaped over the table and grabbed Pete.

While I stood astonished and paralyzed, a similar Beretta appeared in Johnny's hand, probably pulled from a similar hiding place. He aimed and fired two shots—Pop! Pop!—into Victor's chest. "Your boys were too macho to want to squeeze our balls when they frisked us," he shouted as he fired four more shots at the guys still holding up Victor. The three of them went down as a group as though they were tethered together.

Everything moved at a fast blur after that. I was still molded to the floor as I saw Sonny smash a kitchen chair and ram a splintered, pointed leg into the space between the jamb and one of the pocket doors. The guards outside began shaking the doors in a futile attempt to force them open, rattling the glass to the breaking point. Johnny had shouted something at me that I couldn't hear before he turned toward the action and aimed his Beretta at the three Renaissance officers struggling with Pete. Lenny was diving into the corner, his face in pain, to retrieve his M16. My feet suddenly broke free of whatever had been holding them to the floor and I turned away, tripped over Victor's body, and almost plowed headlong into the wall. Then loud, rapid explosions of automatic rifle fire began behind me as I ran down the semidark corridor, not caring about what was going on back there, only wanting to get away, to get to someplace safe.

CHAPTER TWENTY-ONE

I sleepwalked and stumbled past a labyrinth of office cubicles, hallway mazes, empty rooms, and locked doors, through semidarkness, then darkness, then twilight with harsh shadows and sharp angles that leaned into the passages before disappearing and allowing my way to become reality again.

I still heard occasional distant gunfire, and the alternating tones indicated that it came from several areas of the complex. There were a few muffled explosions, like suppressed detonations from somewhere in the building. I passed the line of cubicles for the second time and was this time conscious that they had been converted to sleeping quarters, probably for the officers. None of the compartments were occupied, and I was surprised that I hadn't seen anyone at all since my…retreat.

That's it; call it something other than it is, give it another name to make it sound less severe. You ran! You're a coward! There's nothing to justify that.

I found myself exhausted from the stress and had no idea where in the building I was. I had to stop. I had to think more clearly, to see if I could still salvage my mind…and my soul.

A narrow hallway with ceiling-mounted bare bulbs every twenty feet led me to a dead-end alcove with two steel doors facing each other. One was locked. The other had a crash bar, and when I pushed on it, the door swung open onto a cement landing and metal stairs leading down. A red globe above the door was the only light. I closed the door, angled my shoulders into the corner, slid down the walls, and let my body go limp. There were no sounds. I didn't know if the battle was over or if I had merely happened upon an isolated section of the building.

So you ran out on your friends—the guys you consider to be brothers—just so you could save your own ass. They could both be dead. All of them could be dead. Why? Why couldn't you stick it out?

They never told me they were going to shoot up the place. I didn't know. It took me by surprise. And what could I do with no weapon?

No! No good. That's not an excuse.

They had a purpose in being here. They had a mission to complete, to get the money and get the rat that killed Madge. They had something tangible to risk their lives for. And they really didn't need me in their way. What the hell was I here for?

Apparently not to show any guts. You were here to show them how you could brag about doing anything to help them get Madge's killers, to help steal from the government, to take what *you* think was a perilous journey, and then to fold up when things got hot. Your loyalty to Johnny and Pete is nothing but bullshit! You should've stayed for them.

I clasped my hands around my knees and drew them to my chin. I could feel my essence slipping into depression. I felt a shiver. Don't let those tremors start; they'll take over and your body will shake uncontrollably like you had some disease. Things were spinning in my brain. I was scared of what I had found out about myself. I had to escape, mentally escape. There was nothing I could do now but let myself lapse into some sort of coma. Like a child, I would put the covers over my head. If I didn't see anything then there was nothing there, nothing looming in the dark recesses of my mind that could devour me. I had to make it safe in there because that is where I was going to live from now on. The Renaissance would find me in this fetal position. I would be the only survivor, and they would look at me as so pathetic that they would leave me here to deteriorate and die alone in the darkness, with failure as my epitaph.

At least Gwen wouldn't know what happened to me. She wouldn't know I died a coward. Gwen! Now I remember. She's in danger. I ran so I could stop that truck full of sarin from reaching its destination. I couldn't let them kill her. I had to stop them. Yes! Yes, that was why I had to get out of there, why I had to survive. My priorities had changed since I had heard the Leader's plan. My loyalty was no longer primarily to Johnny and Pete; it had shifted to her. That's what was inside, what unknowingly threw that switch—the flight switch, and the run-to-fight-another day switch that gave someone that precious extra time to think about it.

In one motion I pushed off the wall and stood. The fog in my head was starting to diminish. There was now a definite reason for the risk. No matter how much you do battle inside your head, you must do something to bring that battle into reality, something to bring it into the open to focus on and vanquish your fears, or they will forever stay locked inside your head and haunt you. I knew what I had to do. I had to blow up that damn truck and kill as many of those insane bastards as I could so it couldn't be used on Gwen and a lot of innocent people. Maybe I would go with it, but it beats dying those thousand deaths in this cold, unforgiving stairwell.

I started down the stairs quickly, but I made a hell of a racket on the metal steps and slowed my pace so the noise wouldn't alert anyone that might be on the other side of the lower door. There was an open grate landing halfway and then the ground floor and another red globe. I didn't hear anything coming from the other side of the door, and it was unlocked.

It was a large vacant room, dark except for the small amount of light through the windows from the courtyard lamps and an open hallway on the right side of the room. It was one of many unused rotting-away rooms I had seen in the building. The old-fashioned plaster on the walls and ceiling was cracked and peeled, and large holes revealed the lath strips underneath. A damp, musty smell permeated these uncared-for areas that had no heat sources to keep out the mold. I tried a steel fire door at the other side of the room, and it was locked. I looked through the keyhole and saw that it closed off a long hall that led to the far end of the building and that was only lit at the other end. I walked to one of the multipaned tall windows and looked into the courtyard. It appeared that I was in the middle of the headquarters building.

The barracks building at the far end had a barricade of tables, bedsprings, and mattresses piled along a forty-foot front and ten feet out from the building, but there didn't appear to be any movement behind the barrier. On the other end of the courtyard, the gates were closed and blocked outside by a van and pickup, both parked lengthwise. To the side, our dorm room and platform were pitch black. The Buick was still parked in front, and I couldn't see very clearly but thought there were bullet holes in the hood and remnants of steam clouding its grille. The Chevy and...*only one* of the M37s were parked in the same spots as I had last seen them. *No, the other wasn't blocked from my view.* There *was* only one. Which M37 was gone? The sarin is on the way to Woodstock? Oh, man, no! I felt a sharp pain in my chest and then tightness. I couldn't tell which truck had the sarin and which had the rifles. Maybe the sarin was still there next to the

Chevy. Maybe they thought the rifles were more important. I had to see before my mind cranked out another twisted session.

As I started down the hall that led back toward the main entrance, I was still astounded at the absence of personnel maneuvering through the building. It was as though the battle lines had been drawn and everyone was waiting at their positions for the next phase to begin. The hall took a ninety-degree turn about twenty feet past the room. My confidence level was climbing, and I felt less cautious as I swung around the corner. I ran face first into a wall and reeled back. Damn, no, the dark shape was a person. I recoiled off the corner of the passage and stood facing Snark. He was wearing a black beret with a brass star pinned in the middle. It was funny that I saw that first instead of the AK47 in his hands.

My caution waned even more, fueled by a surge of urgency. I leaped forward and grabbed hold of the rifle. My sudden lunge knocked Snark off balance and we fell, bounced off a wall, and landed on the floor. As I tried to wrestle the AK47 away from him, I was aware of someone standing near us.

"Jimmy! Jimmy, is that you?"

I looked up and saw Red hovering over us. He also held an AK47. I relaxed my grip in astonishment and was instantly tossed against the base of the opposite wall. Snark jumped to his feet and pointed his rifle at me.

"This is that guy that said he was a runner," Snark shouted. "You know him?"

"Yes," Red said. "He's one of us." Red reached down, grasped my hand, and yanked me to my feet. "He's OK."

"What…? What's…?" I couldn't compute the two of them standing there, Red alive and partnered with a member of the Renaissance. My mind was going again, playing tricks, ready to dive back under the covers.

"Relax, Jim," Red said as he grasped my shoulder. "I'm not a ghost. And he won't shoot you." He tilted his head at Snark. "He's on our side."

Snark lowered his weapon and stuck out his hand. "Special agent Sam Clark, FBI."

I absentmindedly shook Snark's hand then looked blankly at Red.

Red looked around the corner I had just turned. "Anybody else with you?" he asked.

"No. No, we split up after…after the fight."

"Fight?"

I pulled myself together and rattled off my recollection of the skirmish. When I finished, I added to my own conscience the fact that I had only left to find the M37s. It worked, and I took another step back to self-confidence. "One of the trucks is gone, and it might be the one with the sarin. I have to stop that sarin from being used," I blurted out. "They're gonna use that shit to kill Gwen and thousands of people."

"Don't worry about it," Red said. "Everything's OK. Look, we were searching this end of the building. You see anything?"

"No. No one. This hall leads to a large room and no farther. There's another hall beyond that, but it has a solid steel fire door blocking it. There's a barrier in front of the barracks building, but I couldn't tell if anyone was behind it."

"That's probably to protect the bikes," Snark said. "They're holed up inside. And they locked off that fire door to protect their flank. The hall beyond leads to the breezeway that joins the two buildings. So, you say the Leader is dead?"

I nodded. "I saw the side of his head blow apart and he went down."

"That puts me in charge. They're probably gathering at the barracks to try to elect someone to replace him, not knowing where I am," Snark-Sam said. "This could work out OK."

Red saw the growing confusion on my face and explained. "Sam has been in deep cover for over a year. He worked himself up to number two in the organization. He was about to get out of here with the dope on these guys when, instead, our little deal was arranged. He stuck around to get us, too, not knowing it was an MI incursion."

"Yeah, like all our intelligence agencies know what each other is doing," Snark said with a smirk.

"Look, the longer we stand here talking, the farther away that sarin is getting," I said. "It's going to kill Gwen and all those people."

"Didn't I tell you to relax?" Red looked around the corner again, then to the other end of the hall. "Do I look dead?"

"Yeah, that's right, you didn't tell me how you got away."

"When Sam found out I was MI undercover, he took me aside like he was gonna personally interrogate me and told me who he was. I told him to continue the ruse and put me in the chamber. When they pumped in the contents of that cylinder, I knew what the symptoms are and did a few twitches and shakes before I played dead. Sam got rid of the others and let me out."

"You mean there's no sarin in those cylinders?" I asked.

Red looked at me like a puppy that had just been scolded. "Do you really think that I—or any sensible member of the military—would even think about allowing that stuff to be put in the hands of psychopaths? There's a slight bit of oxygen in each tank to give the illusion of something initially escaping into the air. That's about it. And who's Gwen, by the way?"

I let out a sigh that drained almost all the air from my lungs. I felt light-headed and leaned against the wall. "Oh, man. Thank you." I leaned forward and hugged Red, then stepped back, embarrassed. "Gwen is usually the only one I hug. I forgot you never met her. She's my girl, and now that she'll be safe in Woodstock, I'll be able to introduce you next time we get together."

"If we can get the hell out of this place," Red said. "If they still think they have the means to make their plan work, and even if the master planner is dead, most of them are surely brainwashed enough to try to carry it out anyway, which makes them dangerous."

"We, or should I say, they," Sam said, "have several well-placed people in vulnerable areas of the Northeast who will immediately, as soon as they think the Woodstock thing is happening, distribute flyers and other literature reporting the Woodstock massacre through the streets and instigating the people to riot and ferment chaos. The members of the press who support their cause will be telephoned, and they'll broadcast the atrocity. People in the SDS, Weathermen, possibly even the Black Panthers, will start an armed resistance. They'll try to take over the streets and control Manhattan and other parts of New York, Boston, Philadelphia, wherever they can make strides. The Renaissance is only a small constituency of those lined up, but they're the vanguard for the start of their revolution. If they fail, nothing further will materialize. So, if we stop them here, it's over.

"The troops that are here are prepared to invade a large area along the Canadian border where they'll try to capture the checkpoints and closeby towns and defend them. They'll round up and hold everyone in those towns as hostages and control their communications. They think that there may be a large number of dissidents who will cross back over the border and join the cause."

"So they'll carry out that part of the plan anyway, thinking that their Woodstock plan went over," Red said.

"Not if I can help it," Sam said. "If I can get back there and assume command, I can confuse things for an hour or so to give you time to get out and get through to my contact. I haven't spoken to him for a couple of weeks. When the Leader locked down the area, he imposed it on everyone, including himself, and of course, we have no phone lines coming into here.

"But the deadline is just about up at the doomsday outpost." He looked at his wristwatch. "The truck is somewhere between posts, waiting for the release time. My contact is the person who will be repainting the truck. He operates a small body shop in the closest town. When he sees the truck, he'll know that something is going down. He won't do anything until he talks to me or to someone I send.

If the missing truck is the one with the bogus sarin, it doesn't matter what becomes of it at this point, but if we can keep it here or dispose of it, no one will have to know what could have happened. Here." Sam handed something to Red. "When he sees this, he'll know you're OK.

"With that main hall locked down, there's no other direct interior route from this building to the barracks," Sam said. "I could get shot by either side if I try to get there over open ground. If we can get to the other truck, I can use it for transportation. Are all your people in that loading area next to the gate?"

"Yeah, I can only guess that everyone is there," Red said. "But the way Jim tells it, they may be spread all over the place. We have a flashlight signal I can use if we get directly across from them. And using that truck would be perfect. Come on, I'll tell you about it when we get there."

"Let's do it," Sam said as we started down the hall. "At least I won't be shot at by your people. I don't know how long this standoff will go on. They're going to want to get these troops out that gate very soon to start up toward their border objectives, but your position controls this side of the gate. On the other hand, they don't want you guys getting out to put out an alarm—or get away with that money. No matter how much some of them proclaim socialism, those capitalistic greenbacks are still first priority. Most of the rank and file care only about their drug trade, and they never intended for that million and a half to leave here with strangers."

CHAPTER TWENTY-TWO

Red and Sam took the lead, their AK47s pointing ahead of us as we twisted and turned through crooked hallways and deserted, musty rooms.

"Excuse me, Snar...or, I mean Sam," I said as we walked. "I just have to know something. Were all of those recent runners that passed through here killed?"

"Only one," Sam said. "I was usually alone and the first to reach them. I'd send them on a different route over the mountain and tell them to forget about this place. It's a longer and more rugged route, but at least they got out alive."

"Good," I said. "I'm glad. I found the knapsack of the one that didn't make it."

"Yeah, well, that was unavoidable. He originally bought into that same recruitment pitch I gave to you. But he soon changed his mind and struck out on his own. One of the patrols found him and opened fire. They were going to deliver his body to town as a warning, but I convinced them to bury him in a local, unused cemetery."

We reached the wall that separated us from the vestibule of the main entrance. Red yanked on the handle of the entrance hall door, and a sliver of the broken upper panes slipped from behind the corrugated cardboard and broke on the floor. Chunks of wood and splinters flew back at us as bullets blasted into the door and jamb. Red twisted away and then moved to the damaged side of the door, poked the barrel of his AK47 into the opening, and sent three quick bursts of fire up the staircase. There was another eruption of fire from above and then another, but none of the bullets hit anywhere near us. Red fired three more volleys. Silence. We waited five minutes before Red ventured into the vestibule, rifle pointing up the stairs. There was no return fire.

"I guess I got the sons of bitches," Red said, still cautiously viewing the darkness at the top of the staircase opposite the one I had climbed earlier.

Sam and I stepped into the vestibule with Red. The smell of cordite stung my nostrils. Sam partially opened one of the heavy outer doors and held it ajar with the barrel of his rifle.

"I wonder which truck that is," I said, pointing to the M37 ten feet away.

"That's the one I drove," Red said. "I remember the bumper number. It's the one with the rifles."

"So the sarin truck did get out," I said with a shiver as I had a fleeting image of what might have happened. "Or, thankfully, the *phony* sarin truck."

"Well, Sam, this is your ride," Red said. "I want them to get these rifles and ammo."

"How come?" Sam asked.

"The barrels were intentionally weakened with chemicals. After firing off a couple of magazines, they'll deteriorate and explode in their faces."

"Perfect," Sam said. "Those are the foot soldiers down there. There's maybe one rifle for every six men. For all their big plans, they're poorly armed. I think they have only one hand grenade, which they used for dry fire practice. No one would sell them any large quantities of arms because they're known as such lunatics, and I would send word to my contact about any deal I heard about so it could be squelched. Your deal was the only one I never got a handle on. They're banking on your rifles and to capture police department and National Guard armories during their takeover of the border towns. The lack of firepower was another reason they couldn't mount an attack against you.

"They'll welcome this truck and whoever is driving it with open arms. I got an idea. You signal your people so they know it's you over here. I'll jump in the truck and head down the yard with you firing at me so the Renaissance will know I'm a friendly. Once I get there, between what confusion I can foster through command and what havoc these rifles will create, maybe you can get out of here. You'll have to fight your way past a small group of guards and sentries as you go."

"What about you?" Red asked.

"I'll be fine," Sam said. "I'll be able to slip away in the confusion later."

"OK, buddy. I got a few tricks up my sleeve waiting over there that will help out." Red pointed toward the platform and then shook Sam's hand. "Good luck. I hope I see you later."

Sam nodded and handed his AK47 to me. I gingerly held out my hands, and they sagged for an instant from its weight. Red smiled and pulled a flashlight from inside his jacket.

Red slid the switch back and forth several times with his thumb, sending a series of light beams across the yard. Within fifteen seconds, a light flashed on and off in various intervals from behind the platform.

"OK," Red said. "They know it's me. They won't fire while you get to the truck. Once you start rolling, we'll open fire and run for our position. The people in the barracks will see our flashes from different parts of the yard, including over there. It should convince them we're all firing at you."

"OK," Sam said. "But be careful running past the gates. The guards will probably open up on you."

"I'm sure our guys will lay down a cover fire, which the boys at the other end will think is being aimed at you." Red looked back at me. "You do know how to fire one of these, don't you?"

"Yeah, I…"

"It's on automatic and ready to go," Sam said. "Just tuck it into your shoulder and pull the trigger. But make sure you don't aim too well. You're supposed to miss me." Then he was gone, sprinting for the M37.

The engine cranked twice before turning over. The din echoed around the walls of the complex, and I could imagine every head within earshot turning to the sound. The gears ground for a split second and the M37 bucked into reverse, revealing three dead bodies stretched out along the cobblestones between the Chevy and where the truck had been parked. They all wore vests.

I'll be damned. The Chevy was still running. There was no visible exhaust, but I could see the slight shake in its body.

"Get ready," Red said. "As soon as he starts forward, head for the platform. When you see me fire, do the same. Good luck, Jimmy."

"Thanks, I'll…"

The M37 lurched forward, just missing the rear of the Chevy. Red was through the doorway with me about ten paces behind. Then he stopped and opened fire. I awkwardly swung my rifle toward the truck before I slid to a stop, turned, and pulled the trigger. The stock vibrated in my shoulder and the burst arced upward. The flash was directly in front of my face and startled me for a moment. I almost twisted my ankle on the irregular cobblestones as I turned back to run.

Red stopped and fired again, and so did I, this time with the stock planted firmly in my shoulder. I turned back to our path just as torrents of fire spilled out the open doorway and window space of the dorm room. We were close now. *God, help me get to those steps.* I heard tin and glass being impacted and bullets ricocheting off the metal gates to our side. Red was at the steps and fired from the hip at the gate, then swung his rifle back down the yard and fired at the truck as he reached the doorway. He leaped over something and disappeared into the dark room.

I tripped on the top step, which probably saved my life. I sprawled across the platform as bullets smashed into the wall between the doorway and window. The return fire above my head was deafening, and I cringed in terror, feeling the vibrations through the concrete, until someone yelled, "Now! Get in here!"

I leaped to my feet and dove through the doorway, over the several mattresses layered across the opening. I hit the floor, and the AK47 jarred loose from my grip just as another round of fire was unleashed from behind me at either the gate or the truck. I tried to push myself up, but my hands rolled out from under me on the hundreds of spent cartridge shells. I kissed the floor before rolling over.

Pete reached back from the side of the doorway and patted my leg. He said something to me, but I waved him off for a moment until my hearing came back. "Good to see you, buddy," he said again. "I was worried when you didn't show up here with us. I was blaming myself for anything that may have happened to you. Sorry I started the ball without thinking about you or anyone else. It's just that when he said…"

"Don't worry about it," I said. "Everything's fine now." I exhaled and wondered if there was some kind of irony in my redemption.

"Welcome home," Johnny said from his crouched position behind a few jagged pieces of glass and remnants of a frame that was once the picture window. "I guess you heard me tell you to cover my back at the hallway before I turned to help Pete. I wasn't thinking about you being unarmed at the time, but I guess you made due. We're really sorry about leaving you and Lenny behind, but it got so confused after that."

Lenny?

"Was that Lenny in the truck?" Johnny asked, twisting toward Red, who was crawling toward the back room. "What the hell does he think he's doing?"

"Lenny?" I asked. "We didn't see Lenny. That was Snark…uh, I mean, Sam. He's an FBI guy."

"FBI?" Johnny asked, confused.

"Later," Red said. He was in the back room, opening a crate. "I'll tell you later. Why did you think Lenny was with us?"

"Because he stayed behind at the top of the staircase and covered us while we got out of the building," Johnny said. "He couldn't run, and everything was so fast and confusing, we figured that's why he stayed. There were Renaissance on the opposite staircase and coming across the courtyard. He had the M16 and probably Pete's shotgun and some ammo. We heard him holding them off as we were crossing the courtyard. They have us pinned down here or we would've tried to get back to him."

"I took care of the resistance on the staircase," Red said. "I heard other firing up there. Maybe he was the one doing the firing. But all the firing stopped inside the stairwell. I don't know…"

"So what's with the truck?" Johnny asked as he jammed a fresh clip into his M16 and slammed it in place with the heel of his hand.

"It has to do with the damaged rifles. I'll explain everything once I'm done setting up," Red said. He was dragging an open crate into the room. "Give me a hand, Mike."

Mike Looney appeared out of the shadows and grabbed the side of the crate, and they slid it to where Johnny crouched.

I acclimated my vision and looked around the room. The lamps on the platform parapets had been destroyed by gunfire, and only a hint of light came from across the courtyard. There were rifle magazines scattered over the floor or stacked near people, and the ejected brass shells and chunks of mortar and plaster looked like part of the design pattern of the floor. Sonny and Pete were on either side of the doorway, both armed with M16s. If I didn't know them by their general appearance, I wouldn't have recognized anyone in the darkness. There were two mattresses, acting like fortification sandbags, held in place with the weight of one of the couches and its pillows across the opening. I strained my eyes and could make out a figure on one of the beds. He moaned, and Mike scrambled back to him. It was Pat, who was apparently wounded.

"How is he?" Johnny asked.

"He'll be all right," Mike said. "All I can see is his shoulder wound. I got him patched up, but he's in pain."

"Maybe we can get him out of here soon, but meantime I'll give him something for the pain in a minute," Red said. "This should help us out."

Red lifted an M60 machine gun from the crate and leaned the barrel against the wall next to Johnny. He pulled out a tripod and assembled it. "It's a good thing there were enough rifles and ammo already unloaded and nobody tried to open these boxes without me deactivating the charges in the lids or somebody would've had a real blast," he said. "Aren't you glad I'm back?"

"By the way, how come no one's surprised to see him alive like I was?" I asked.

"Because you were probably the only one left who wasn't told that there was no poison gas," Johnny said. "Only Red, Lenny, and I knew from the beginning. We knew he couldn't have been killed. We figured he was more than capable of finding a way out and back here. We filled in everyone else later."

"You mean you didn't even tell Pete?" I asked.

"We wanted everyone to think that the deal was going down with the real stuff. There was less of a chance of anything slipping beforehand or in the heat of passion."

"Like when Pete…That was good shooting, man," I said. "You sure got that bastard." Pete only nodded. "So I guess the trucks weren't wired to explode either," I surmised.

"Just some Lenny bullshit to keep them guessing," Johnny said as he moved back from the window. "Since we knew that what was in the trucks was also bullshit, we left them when we pulled back to here. They managed to get the one truck out the gate and knock out the Buick before we could set up."

Red lifted the M60 into place on the tripod, and he and Johnny moved the assembly to the corner of the window. He slid the cocking handle back, then forward, strung a bandolier of 7.62-mm bullets out of a case, set the end cartridge into the gun, and slammed the cover shut. "There's surprise number one," Red said. He duckwalked to the back room.

"I'm worried about Lenny," Johnny said. "I haven't heard any fire from over there since you guys got here."

"Maybe he's low on ammo and conserving it," I said. "If you can cover me, I'll try to get back across to him." I only calculated what I had said after the words had been uttered. Gwen was safe, and I was back in the fold, with my metabolism pumped up from the sprint across the yard. So why not try to square things with Lenny? He was beginning to warm up to me. If he could be made to feel indebted in some small way, then maybe it would wash away the embarrassment I had caused him. Everything would be right again.

"How you gonna get across…"

"Let him go," Red shouted from the back room. "He did good getting here. We can cover him with the M60. They won't know what hit them when we open up with that." Red was back in the room and was holding an M79 grenade launcher in one hand and a 40-mm grenade in the other. "And this."

"I'll go with him," Pete said. "I don't know what it is, but I got to see that bastard's body to be sure I really got him."

"OK, listen." Red pointed at Pete and me. "Here's the plan. I'll keep the gate guards busy with the M60. They'll have their heads buried in the sand. Once you get across, start up the Chevy. It looked like it wasn't damaged."

"It was still running," I said. "I'm sure of it."

"OK, good. Leave it running, get up the stairs and get Lenny. Get him down to the Chevy and pull over to the other platform just out of sight of the gate. We'll open up again, and I'll see if I can blast a hole through the gate with a couple of grenades. We'll get Pat over to you, so at least the wounded can get out. Whoever's left walking will try to commandeer another vehicle outside the walls."

"That sounds mighty ambitious," Johnny said. "And what do you think the troops at the other end will be doing all this time?"

"If we're lucky, Sam will…"

"Who's Sam?"

"I'll tell you in a minute," Red said impatiently. "Hopefully he'll keep everyone down there from responding and we can get the hell out of here."

CHAPTER TWENTY-THREE

The heavy chatter of the M60 was probably the first thing that the gate guards realized was different about the renewed gunfire. Then the heavier-caliber bullets began slamming into their vehicles and off the bars of the gate. I saw a dark figure in the cramped space between the van and pickup fall and become lodged between the bumpers. I jerked my head back behind the brick retaining wall that sheltered part of the steps and readied myself for another mad dash. Pete was poised behind me. We both carried M16s and six extra magazines.

The silence was sudden but welcome to my hyper state of mind. I leaped to the ground and broke into full stride, head down, not looking at the gate and only raising my head when I was sure I was halfway across the yard. Another exchange of gunfire rattled behind us. I didn't look back but could hear Pete's footsteps after the firing stopped. My second trip, and this time I was the lead man. What a rush! I waved Pete on and stopped at the Chevy. The engine *was* still running. I opened the door, slid in, maneuvered the car around the bodies, and faced it toward the platform that flanked this side of the gate, then got out and followed Pete through the entrance of the headquarters building. No one had fired at us from the barracks. Sam was doing his part.

I wedged pieces of the damaged jamb and other debris under the front door to keep it ajar and allow some light into the pitch-black stairwell—and for a quick exit. Pete was up a few steps, staring cautiously into the darkness,

"Lenny!" I shouted, now fairly certain there were no enemies above. "Lenny, it's Pete and Jim."

There was no answer, and I hoped against what seemed obvious as I passed Pete and took the steps two and sometimes three at a time. We both seemed to remember at the same time about the flashlights in our pockets. Both beams scoured the steps ahead of our race to the top. There was a body sprawled along the wall. Was it…no, it was Jerome. I passed him. The pocket doors were torn apart and shattered by bullet holes. There was no glass or upper frames. The doors were parted, leaving about a three-foot opening. A rifle barrel was lying on the floor in the opening.

I pushed what was left of both doors further apart and saw Lenny on the floor behind the rifle. I squatted and checked his pulse while sweeping the flashlight beam over his body. He had blood-soaked makeshift bandages fashioned from the cloth of his jacket tied around two wounds on his back. He was dead. Damn! If only we had known he was up here when we were down there before.

I rolled him over, and Pete shone his light on the body. He was in a large pool of blood but was no longer bleeding from his wounds. There were several injuries to his chest and one ragged hole in the side of his neck. Damn! Damn! Damn! It probably was him firing at the opposite staircase before. I was sure of it. He helped us get out of here and we didn't even know he needed our help. I guess he just couldn't bullshit his way out of this one.

"I don't believe it!" I hadn't realized that Pete's flashlight beam was gone until I heard his shout. "He's not here!" Pete yelled. "He's gone."

I stood and moved to the overturned table and scattered broken chairs. There were three bodies on the floor behind where the table had stood. They all wore berets, and none had on a red vest. "I saw you get him. I saw…Maybe they hauled away his body. You know, like he was a martyr or something like that to them."

"No," Pete said. "I had this gut feeling that he wasn't dead."

I shone my light at the bodies of Victor and his two companions heaped in a pile. "At least Johnny got the guy who actually did it," I said.

"He may have done it, but this guy," Pete pointed to the floor where the Leader had fallen, "was responsible. He's guiltier than that asshole. I gotta get him again."

"That's gonna be difficult," I said. "In fact…Damn, if he's back in the barracks area, then Sam, the FBI guy we told you all about before our little race over here, won't be in charge like he thought he'd be."

It sounded like a stadium full of cheering fans or Times Square on New Year's Eve. It couldn't be from our guys. There had to be at least a hundred voices bellowing. I ran to the window and looked toward the barracks. They were pouring out the two doorways, filling up the area between the building and the barricade, mingling among the motorcycles. Most had AR15s. Others were unloading the last of the weapons from the M37. That wasn't what they were cheering about. Something was happening.

Then I saw why. He stepped from the closest doorway and waved his raised hand in acceptance of their applause. He wore the red vest, and most of his head was wrapped in something white with a crimson blotch on the right side that matched his vest. The Leader had been reincarnated.

Pete raised his rifle and tried to smash the window. They were double-thick reinforced panes, and the butt bounced off the glass several times before the pane bowed out, shattered, and finally broke free and flew into the courtyard. By the time Pete had swung the barrel around to fire, the leader had been hustled back into the building and his followers had let out a hail of fire in our direction. More of the panes shattered, this time inward, raining shards of glass on me as I hit the floor. Pete stood defiant in a bricked space between the windows.

"Hold your fire, Pete," I yelled. "You can't get him. He's back inside. Let them think they got us."

Then the M60 opened up and I could hear ricochets off the cobblestones and then off the other end of the building. I bent below the window line and moved down a few yards before looking out. There were two new Renaissance lying face down below and others streaming between the barricade and the headquarters building into an area out of my line of sight.

"They're coming for us," I yelled. "We gotta get to the Chevy to protect it. It's our only way out of here."

"I gotta get him," Pete mumbled. "That's why I'm here."

"You can't now. We have to get out of here. That's the only way you'll get another chance." I grabbed his arm and pulled. "If we get downstairs, we can pin them in a crossfire between us and the other guys, to give us time to get into the Chevy and get back across. It won't be long before they realize it's safer to come through the interior and unlock that fire door at the other end of the building."

Pete finally turned, and we hurried past Lenny's body. Pete retrieved his shotgun before following me down the stairs. *We have to recover Lenny's body*, I told myself. It'll be only right we bring him home for burial. The M60 began firing again as we reached the vestibule. I heard its slugs tearing along the lower level of the building and windows about twenty yards from us.

"They're close," I yelled.

I leaned out the door when a second covering round of M60 fire started, and I emptied the contents of my magazine into the now retreating Renaissance troops.

About thirty of them eventually made it back to the barracks and the safety of the barricade. They left almost a third of that lying on the cobblestones. I had let my adrenalin control my actions, but now, looking at them lying there, I was aware and, for a split second, ashamed, that some could've been put there by me. I felt empty, then queasy, before remembering what they had done to Lenny and that runner and that they were doing their best to kill me. What I did wasn't wrong. I had to do it. And I would have to keep doing it.

"Pete! Open the trunk of the car and then get behind the wheel. I'm gonna get Lenny's body to bring home."

"Why? What…"

"Wouldn't you want to bring Johnny home if he got it?"

"Yeah, I guess. But Lenny was out to get you."

"Nah. We made up."

"OK. You want me to help?"

"No, I can handle it. Keeping the Chevy safe to get to the other guys is more important." I left my M16 leaning against the door and bolted back up the stairs. Lenny wasn't too big or heavy of a guy. I dragged him to the edge of the stairs, positioned myself a few steps down, and maneuvered him over my shoulders into a fireman's carry.

I stayed close to the wall and leaned slightly backward to balance the weight against gravity as I descended. I had helped him up these stairs, and now I was helping him down. It was good I was doing this. He wasn't really gonna kill me. We were becoming friends. *I just knew it.* It would've been all right.

I would bounce off the banister every few feet before regaining my balance and continuing on. There was only sporadic gunfire outside, and I hoped I could get Lenny out of here before someone found his way through the maze of hallways and reached us. I made it to the bottom and stopped to look through the entryway. The Chevy was chugging and spitting as it lumbered by me. I stood helplessly watching the open trunk lid bouncing freely, as if it was waving goodbye at me, as the car headed toward the barracks.

"Pete! What are you doing?" I stood there with Lenny's body across my shoulders, and he suddenly felt heavy.

CHAPTER TWENTY-FOUR

I was over my amazement instantly and now became concerned with what was Pete's obsession to kill the Leader. I backed into the far wall and slid down, depositing Lenny's body gently on the floor. I grabbed my M16 and stepped out the doorway. The Chevy was about three-quarters of the way to the barricade when it suddenly bucked and its nose pointed downward. It rolled a few more feet and coasted to a halt. *It happened.* It finally ran out of gas.

I began running toward the car as the driver's door swung open. Surprisingly, no one had fired at it. Maybe they thought it was another of their members. Pete stumbled out into view, M16 in one hand and sawed-off shotgun in the other.

"Get behind the car!" I yelled. "Use it for cover."

"It's some of them," someone from behind the barricade shouted.

I pulled the trigger as I ran, but nothing happened. Damn it, I forgot to put in a fresh magazine. *This isn't the movies, idiot. You don't have a couple thousand rounds to fire before reloading.* I reached Pete as both he and some of the Renaissance opened fire. He slipped behind the Chevy as a hail of bullets peppered the exposed top of the open lid and slammed it down at us. I fumbled out another magazine and reloaded as Pete returned fire.

"Are you still convinced you can get to him?" I shouted.

He said nothing and seemed to be concentrating only on wiping out the entire Renaissance army.

"If you try something stupid, I'm not following you. You'll be dead and he'll still be walking around." I moved to the opposite side from Pete, and a line of slugs blasted fragments of cobblestone into my hands and body. The sting of the debris seemed to deflate my high, and I felt trapped behind this flimsy screen of glass and tin. *What the hell did I do?*

As I ducked back from another shower of stone chips, I saw our salvation. The M37 that had delivered the rifle cargo was facing us about twenty yards away, at the far end of the barricade where there wasn't any activity. If only we could...An explosion boomed in front of us. The firing from the barracks stopped and I looked out quickly. There was a smoking hole about thirty feet in front of the barricade, and a few of the mattresses were on fire. Red and his grenade launcher! Yeah, it must have been.

"Pete, quick, let's get to the truck while they're still ducking," I said as I pointed toward the M37. "We can use it to replace the Chevy."

Pete nodded, and I was relieved that he was thinking sensibly again. At least, I hoped he was.

I anticipated they were too busy with the fire or worried about being shelled to have any immediate concern with us. I took off for the truck. The mattress fire was now lighting the courtyard around the center of the barricade and cast an eerie shimmering glow on the barracks building.

"Water! Get water! Move those bikes out'a there!" was being shouted as we reached the M37. I jumped through the open door into the driver's seat. *Hallelujah!* The keys were in the ignition and I started the engine. Pete couldn't get the passenger door open and wiggled in through the open window as I jammed the shift lever into gear and released the clutch. As we started forward, I saw movement in the rear view mirrors. I shifted gears as Pete leaned out the window. The shotgun roared. He pumped it and the spent shell bounced off the inside of the windshield just as the sawed-off thundered a second time.

Then bullets from the M60 flashed past us and we were home free. I guided the truck to the rear edge of the platform and against the building where it would be out of the line of fire from all directions. The M60 shifted direction and lay down a field of fire at the gate.

"Let's go!" I yelled, hoping someone in the room would hear me over the noise. "Let's get the hell out of here."

There was a loud *poof* from behind the platform. The gates exploded, bent outward, and slammed into the two vehicles behind them. But the site was still blocked. *Poof!* Another detonation. The gates twisted, and the van left the ground with a gaping hole in its side panel, then toppled and crashed onto its other side. There was a glow from inside, and then flames leaped through the fissure. There still wasn't enough room to get out of this goddamn courtyard, not even if I pulled out and rammed the mess. The bottom of the van was facing us, and I could see the floor smoking. Then the fire seeped through rust holes or conduits, and I could see them lapping at the fuel tank. Ramming was definitely out of the question.

"Let's get out of here," I shouted. My door had no clearance to open, so I squeezed through the passenger window opening after Pete. I reached back in for the ignition key and my rifle and then followed Pete. He was carrying his two weapons as he climbed over the hood. We were both on the platform when the explosion from the van knocked us off balance and back toward the loading door. There probably wasn't enough gas in the tank to produce a major bang, but there was enough to surprise me: I expected to bounce off the ribbed metal door but instead found myself on the concrete floor of the rear storeroom. Someone reached from the side of the opening and dragged me out of the heat and light being produced by the fire. I saw Red rush out and drag Pete deeper inside the room.

"What in the hell were you guys thinking?" Johnny shouted from over me.

I looked over at Pete lying a few feet away from me and then said, "We thought the truck would be more useful than the Chevy. It ran out of gas, so we couldn't have used it anyway."

"My two heroes," Johnny said sarcastically. "You could've gotten yourselves killed."

"Yeah, like Lenny," I said as I stood and felt a pain along the entire side of the leg I had landed on.

"You're kidding! Are you sure?"

"Yes." I looked at Pete, who was now standing. "And neither of us accomplished our mission. Lenny's still over there." I pointed at both buildings. "And the Leader is over there. Alive."

"What?"

"It's true. We saw him from upstairs before they fired at us," Pete said. "Thanks for covering for me, Jim, but the truth is I drove the Chevy over there to try to get the son of a bitch again. Jim got my head back in order and got us out of there. I owe him."

"Forget it," I said. "How are we getting out of here?"

Red was slipping a grenade into the open M79. It looked like he was loading a wide-mouth single-barrel shotgun. "I'd like to try to blast again, but this is my last shell. Somebody screwed up when they packed my supplies. That's why I could only waste one to help get you guys out of trouble. Their position down there is out of range. You were lucky some of the hot fragments made it to the mattresses." He snapped the M79 shut and locked it. "So I needed the rest for the gate, but I don't know if another blast will be enough."

Shouts grew louder from the gate, and the shimmering of the flames against the floor surface began to fade. We all leaned forward and into the doorway to get a better view. Dozens of people were tossing dirt with shovels, buckets, and cardboard slats on the dwindling fire of the fuel tank and its streams of spillage. When that was out, others began appearing with buckets of water and spilling them through openings in the overturned van and onto its interior fire. The air was filled with hissing and billows of smoke. They had formed a bucket brigade and were hauling water from the river.

Red raised the M79 to his shoulder.

"No, wait," I said. One of the bucket brigade wore a white straw hat. "They're people from the town."

"But they're helping," Red said.

"No, look." The fire was out, and only the small amount of light from the still-functioning lamps in the courtyard illuminated the scene. The buckets were discarded, and the townspeople, both male and female, were being made to file along the gate opening by a handful of Renaissance soldiers. They were lined shoulder to shoulder facing us along the breadth of the twisted gates, which were lying partially on the ground but still attached to the walls by their lower hinges. An armed soldier hunched behind every fifth or sixth person. "They're being used as shields."

Flashes over the shoulders of the hostages and the spray of bullets drove us back out of the opening. I could hear cries and shouts from the civilians and bullets striking harmlessly somewhere behind us in the immensity of the storeroom.

"Hold your fire," Red shouted as he rushed through the doorway into the dorm room and pulled Sonny back from the handle of the M60. "They're noncombatants."

"But they're shooting at us," Sonny said.

"Not them. Not the ones in front," Red said. "We can't be involved in a civilian massacre. That's what I came here to try to prevent."

"What about up there?" Sonny asked, pointing at the headquarters building.

We were all in the dorm room now, on our hands and knees, wallowing among the spent shells and debris and looking across the yard. Silhouettes were moving against the sky, backlit by the town's lights and crossing the rooftop.

"How the hell did they get up there?" Red pondered. "Mike, keep an eye on the barracks in case they start moving in from that direction."

Mike was beside the entrance door in a spot where he could observe the far end of the yard. He nodded in acknowledgement. Johnny returned to the loading door, and I settled behind Sonny and Red.

"I don't know if you can reach them, but give it a try," Red said as he patted Sonny's shoulder.

Sonny swung the M60 ninety degrees on the tripod and began firing. The slugs were only striking the second floor. He jerked the handle down into his lap, and the barrage of bullets reached the stone ledges of the roofline, smashing into the patina-green copper gutters but not reaching the group. It was enough to make them hit the deck.

"They're moving up into the small buildings on our side of the yard," Mike announced. "Looks like they're gonna try to leapfrog down to the back of our building."

"Well, that's it," Red said. "We're about to be surrounded."

CHAPTER TWENTY-FIVE

"Can they get on top of our roof?" Sonny asked, pointing into the air.

"No," Red said. "It's pitched, not flat like the main buildings. They can get up there, but there wouldn't be much tactical advantage. It's clad in copper, very slippery, and they'd make a hell of a racket, which would warn us."

"Damn, this is my fault for flying off the handle. I dug us a hole that's getting harder and harder to get out of," Pete said.

"We're all in this together," Red consoled. "Sam said they weren't going to let us out of here, no matter what happened. So let's just try to think our way out."

"What are we gonna do?" Pete asked.

"This front looks like a standoff for now," Red said. "We can defend it, providing they don't shift their forces." He turned to Pat, who was sitting on the edge of the bed. "Pat, can you handle the machine gun?"

Pat adjusted the crosspiece of his sling and stood. "No sweat. I still got one good arm and I'm getting tired of lying around. Those codeine pills you had in your medical kit helped a lot."

"OK, you're on. Every time those jokers on the roof lift their heads, give them a few rounds until they duck again. But remember, under no circumstance do you fire at those civilians. Understand?"

"Yeah. But just let one of those Renaissance guys stick his puss a little closer than they are now." Pat inched his way behind the M60 as Sonny slid out of the way.

Red slipped on a padded mitt and changed barrels on the M60. The barrel became so hot that it could warp and needed to be interchanged during heavy usage.

"Sonny, grab your rifle and the AK47 I brought back and cover from the loading door," Red said. "Mike, you're good where you are. Use the other AK47 if you need it. Cover each other in crossfire and let the M60 swing either way. If Pat gets into a situation where he needs someone to feed the M60, one of you jump in. And the three musketeers can come with me. I'm expecting an attack through the rear of the storehouse."

We followed Red into the dark of the long, empty storeroom. He carried an M16 and a red lens flashlight in case someone was close enough to see a regular beam. He had unloaded the M79 and left it and the 40-mm grenade on one of the crates to the side of the doorway. Johnny and I had M16s, and Pete carried his shotgun with his rifle slung over his shoulder. There were no windows, and only Red's red beam guided the way. Our footsteps echoed through the emptiness, and, together with the eerie red tint and constant dripping of water somewhere nearby, I felt like we were exploring a cavern. I looked back and could see a faint gray rectangle that was the loading dock doorway.

We came upon a stockade of mostly crates, supplemented with broken desks and tables, piled across the thirty-foot width of the room. Red slowly moved the light across the rampart. It was about four feet tall and was constructed with a half dozen openings that looked like gun ports just below the top layer.

"This is where I spent those hours when I disappeared," Red said. "This and reconnoitering wherever I could. I found all these empty crates and discarded office furniture just sitting here waiting for me." He shone the light at two flat boxes with rope handles. "There are plenty of loaded magazines for the M16s in one box. And…" He opened the lid of the second box. There were a dozen hand grenades in compartments. "These will back us up, if needed. We should be able to hold them off with small arms and my other surprise." He picked up the box of hand grenades and moved to one end of the stockade.

"This is my control center." A wooden crate was set up as a station for a variety of levers and switches. Red flicked one and the area twenty feet in front of us lit up. There were spotlights mounted and facing away from us just below the ceiling on both walls. He activated a second switch and the area at the far end of the room became illuminated. There were two large sliding doors occupying most of the far wall, and as soon as they appeared out of the darkness, we could see the levered handles being jiggled against the padlocks that held them closed.

"They're trying to get in," Red said. He turned off the spotlights and shone his flashlight for us to find our way. "Everyone spread out and grab a hole. Don't fire until I turn on the lights at that end. If we can take out enough of them, maybe they'll back off and we can negotiate to get the hell out of here. Good luck."

"What are those other controls for?" I asked from my firing post, the next down from Red's position.

"Claymore antipersonnel mines," Red said. He turned off the flashlight. "A very good deterrent in a small space against an advancing enemy."

I bent forward and leaned on the ledge created by the wooden carton and a smaller wooden box that I used to rest the barrel of my M16. I pushed the butt deep into my shoulder, rested my cheek on the stock, and girded myself for yet another test of my resolve. This is what you came to do, to prove you can do it. *How do you like it? It's not very pretty. Not what I would ever want to do again.* I trust in Red. He'll get us out of here. I know he will. Just do what he tells you.

There was a deafening explosion; the metal latch and handle hit the floor with a clang, and then one of the sliding doors opened. Low voices were spreading across the width of the room, their words indistinct but growing a little closer. Then a few flashlight beams appeared. The lock of the second door was shot off. A click from Red's post and suddenly there stood the owners of the voices, exposed and petrified in the blinding light. I remembered how I felt when the bridge lights glared on me, and I empathized with their surprise and shock. But they had no riverbank to escape down.

I squeezed the trigger, and our barricade came alive with the ragged sounds of individually controlled gunfire. Those exposed in the glaring white rectangle were falling. Some ran to the sides and clung to the walls, but they found no cover and tried to fire their weapons at the unknown enemy in the darkness before them. There were a few bursts and I heard bullets strike the wood of our barrier; one of the spotlights disappeared in a bright flash and flume of smoke. They had no choice but to withdraw, and those that could raced back through the safety of the two open doorways. There was silence and a click from where Red stood, and there was also darkness again. Round one was over; I changed magazines.

I heard a moan from the far end, and I thought of Lenny. I wondered, and then hoped, he hadn't lain there suffering and moaning when we could have helped him. No, we would've heard him. He would've called to us when he heard familiar voices. He had probably been killed by the last exchange of fire between him and those on the other staircase. I was sure he never wanted to be a hero, but after this is over and we evaluate everything, he will definitely be one to us. We, and mostly I, still had to get his body home for a proper burial.

The moaning from the far end seemed closer this time, much closer than before. Was someone sneaking up on us? I tensed and slid my finger into the trigger guard.

"Red," a voice from the area of the moaning called softly. "It's Sam."

"Hold your fire," Red said. "Sam, live fire diversion practice for one minute." Then Red's words shifted to us. "Everyone, fire high, pace out fifteen seconds each, starting with Johnny. Go!"

Johnny's M16 rattled off a series of bursts, then Pete, Red, and me. We attracted a spattering of return fire, but very little struck the barricade.

"OK, I'm in," Sam said as he slapped the bottom of the crate in front of Red. I could hear Red helping him climb over the obstruction.

"Glad you knew what I was talking about," Red said.

"I crawled under a lot of live fire at Quantico," Sam said. "Thanks for the cover. When you guys initially opened fire, I hit the deck and then crawled as far forward as I could in the confusion, and then some more after the lights went out. I almost got tangled up in your Claymore wires. I'm thankful you didn't blow those off in my face."

"Glad you could join us," Red said. He turned on the red lens, keeping it below the crest of the barricade, and I saw that Sam still wore his Snark beret. "But why'd you desert? They on to you?"

"No, but the Leader is back in charge."

"Yeah, we know. They saw him all bandaged up."

"That head wound made him nuttier than he was," Sam said. "His priorities have changed. He's delaying the attack on the Canadian border until he takes care of you guys. He knows the sarin got out, and he's convinced that it will complete that part of the mission. I assured him that your body was on board." He pointed at Red. "As you know, we didn't leave any witnesses at the chamber to contradict me.

"Because we're so close to the border, he figures that he has time left to get you and still get enough troops up north for the second phase of his plan. He wants that money back, and he wants the guy who shot him, and he won't stop until it's done. They're all high from a variety of stuff—weed, LSD, some H. They're all hopped up, and they'll keep attacking until they win."

"Let him come and get me," Pete said loudly from the darkness. "It'll give me another crack at him."

"Take it easy," Red said. "Voices carry in empty spaces. Talk low."

Don't worry," Sam said in Pete's direction. "You gave him a nasty wound and he's going to need proper medical treatment pretty soon."

"So, do you know their attack plan for us?" Red asked.

"They got troops up on the headquarters roof, and they'll try to pin you down in your room..."

"Our M60 will keep them busy," Red said.

"There's steel ladders running off the roof on the outside wall of that building. That's how they got up there, and some of them will use the ladders to join up with and reinforce the guards at the gate. Then there's the group I *volunteered* to lead through here, about thirty-five strong, less the six or seven you just took out. There are another fifty sneaking up the outside wall of this building to catch you in a pincers movement. They'll be backed up by the bikers, who he's holding in reserve."

"Too bad I built this defense so far from the room. We could've interchanged our firepower between the two," Red said. "Well, it'll just take a lot more running back and forth. Johnny and Pete can go back to the room and get that M60 moved to the entrance door where it can cover the approach of the troops from outside this wall. The gate crew will probably stop firing soon so they don't hit their own troops coming up that way, but have Sonny and Mike stay by the loading door to watch them. Sam, grab this box of grenades and take over their position."

"Here, take my rifle," Pete said to Sam. "I'll either use the machine gun or my sawed-off if they get close enough."

Red pointed the subdued red beam at Johnny and Pete and they soon faded out of view, navigating in the dark toward that gray rectangle in the distance. Red placed the red light on his workbench and cast it upon his array of switches. I smiled, remembering the flashlight that had been like a companion to me during my trip. Crazy, how someone will cling to anything out of loneliness, make an inanimate object into a friend when he has no human companionship. Or maybe I was the only someone to do such a thing.

We settled back into our defense just as a volley of gunfire erupted from the sliding doors and tore into our heavy wooden stockade. I cringed away from my gun port, a knee-jerk reaction to the image of a lucky round finding my head.

"That's it!" Red said. "Keep firing those AR15s, boys. Heat up those barrels and get ready for a big surprise." I heard the familiar click of one of his switches, but nothing happened. There was another click and the same result. "What the hell! The lights won't go on."

"They may have shut down the generator that controls this building," Sam said. "Get ready, they'll be..."

A mix of rebel yells and the screaming and bellowing of threats hit us like the vibration from a high-wattage speaker system and sounded as frightening as the accompanying gunfire. They were charging toward us out there in the darkness. Sam and I opened fire. Red was waiting. It looked like he was trying to judge their rate of advance. Then the explosions thundered back at us and the screaming came from pain rather than to provoke fear.

Their gunfire persisted over the sounds of agony, flashes lighting up the sides of the room about thirty yards ahead. Explosions that differed in tone from the Claymores vibrated from each wall. Grenades? Yes, Sam's grenades were seeking out those that weren't mowed down by the Claymores. And then, finally, retreat—or annihilation—I couldn't tell which in the dark. I only knew their gunfire had stopped.

I barely had time to load a fresh magazine and catch a breath when I heard the roar of motorcycle engines. And there were flames! Streams of fire roared out of the door openings. Molotov cocktails were coming at us in the hands of two motorcycle riders trying to weave through the piles of bodies. It looked like a circus act coming out of the darkness of the wings and heading for us, as if we were the audience in the stands. We opened fire and they went down. One of the riders hurled his gas bomb before being thrown from his machine. The Harleys slid toward us in a shower of sparks.

One veered sideways, its rider tangled in the structure and waving and pumping the fire in his hand, trying to get rid of his Molotov. The bike smashed into a wall and bounced back into the center of the room. It and its rider erupted into a fireball. The other bike plowed into the center of the barricade and pulverized the crates at the exact time the thrown Molotov struck but didn't explode. The simultaneous action created a five-foot-wide corridor of flames through the center of our fortification and knocked me to the ground.

"Get back!" Red shouted. "Back to the room."

I jumped up and turned to run as I heard a diminished chorus of rebel yells. The twisted motorcycle was still bouncing and skidding ahead of me. I could see it very clearly in the light of the burning barricade. I could see all the way back to the loading door and entrance to the dorm room. I thought I heard…Yes, the M60 was firing. They were all firing. And the motorcycle had stopped, coming to rest against a wall. As I passed it, I turned back and found that neither Red nor Sam was with me.

Sam was hurling grenades, and the flash of the explosions overpowered the radiance of the burning barricade. Red was still at his post, holding a lever device in each hand. I changed magazines as I started back. The cement floor shook, and a detonation louder than any of those I had heard before ripped apart both walls in front of the barricade. Red was now running toward me, and sections of the walls of the storeroom were collapsing, tumbling in a cascade toward the floor. Then I saw Sam behind Red and something following him, something on the floor. It looked like a slithering snake, but there were little branches popping to its sides. It was a crack in the cement, running back from the barricade. The ceiling above our stockade groaned, belched a loud raspy sound, and followed the walls down into the room in a cloud of dirt and rubble so large that it crushed the stockade and extinguished the fire.

"Come on. Get the hell out of here in case we didn't get them all," Red said as he ran by me.

I took one more look at the smoldering heap of pulverized masonry and sheets of twisted copper, glinting green in the courtyard light now filtering in, and I knew that no one was going to follow us.

CHAPTER TWENTY-SIX

"What the hell did you set off?" I asked Red when I caught up to him outside the dorm room.

"C4 on the support beams in front of our position, set off electronically," Red said. He came up behind Sonny at the loading entrance and surveyed the situation. "It was my last defense. I had to wait until the last of them got close enough before…"

The M60 drowned out the rest of his words. I moved up behind Red and could see the flash from the machine gun muzzle as it fired from the entrance door at somewhere beside us on the outer wall. As Red had calculated, no firing was coming from the gates. The townspeople were gone, and there was no one at all in the framework of the fallen gates and damaged vehicles.

Then I saw a movement around the opening near the brick retaining wall. There were figures stirring, just barely in our field of vision, and disappearing somewhere along the wall that joined the gate post to the stairs.

"They're moving up from the gate," Red said. He quickly moved to the far side of the loading doorway and wedged himself sideways behind the narrow post with his weapon pointed toward them. "Sonny, stay where you are. Jim and Sam, get on the ground. Fire from a prone position so you're less of a target."

I sprawled behind Sonny's legs, with only my upper body exposed in the opening, and planted my elbows on the cement for solid support. The M60 was quiet, and I guess I began to think like Red because that told me that the first attack was coming from the direction of the gate.

And they came, swinging away from the wall and charging at the steps. Our four M16s and two from the picture window opened up. Their next formation fanned into echelons that wheeled out into the courtyard from the base of the wall and swept around toward the platform. They fired as they ran, and most got off only a burst or two before they were knocked backward or fell forward below the edge of the platform. But they kept coming, and some made it to the steps, where they met the wrath of the M60 from close range. Bullets tore through them, making ragged shreds out their backs and launching them into a backward swan dive onto the cobblestones or skidding onto the platform. Suddenly, something came flying from around the corner where Red stood. It hit off the lower sill of the window frame and rolled onto the platform, where it bounced erratically like a pinball being driven around the surface.

"Grenade!" Red shouted as he flung himself across the opening and landed next to Sam and me. I saw Sonny leap away from the doorway, and I covered up just as the grenade exploded and tore both upper portions of the wooden door jambs off the walls, raining a shower of splinters on us. I felt Red push off me, and I saw that the bodies on the platform had absorbed or deflected most of the grenade blast. Then, above the bodies, legs suddenly appeared all over the platform.

I lifted myself halfway to my feet before I saw Red swinging his chattering rifle in a one-eighty arc across the area. He charged onto the platform, blocking our field of fire. I sidestepped around him and opened fire at the two Renaissance that were still standing next to the front door. *No M60 fire. What happened to Johnny and Pete? Did the grenade get them?* I only hit one, and the other fired at me with his bolt-action hunting rifle. The single shot buzzed past my ear, and Red cut him down before I could react.

Damn, I had actually heard the bullet go past my ear, and I realized that if my adversary had had an automatic rifle, I'd be dead. Bullets began to ricochet off the platform. They were firing from the rooftop. Red backpedaled into the storeroom and fired one last burst before his clip ran out. I heard the hood of the M37 being pounded and flexed. Then the roof of the Buick buckled. They were climbing over the parked vehicles onto the platform. The rooftop gunfire stopped.

There they were, two of them. Red was in the way, slapping a magazine into his M16. Then two more appeared. The first two were cut down from someone in the room. I hadn't noticed that Sonny had moved into the dorm room. He leaped out the window opening and fired at the flood of Renaissance trying to overwhelm Red. The last two attackers had now become six and were all over the platform. I opened fire blindly to the side of Red, and one fell next to him. Red and Sonny were mixed in such close proximity with the mob of Renaissance that no one could fire without hitting one of their own. They were struggling hand to hand, slipping and sliding on the bloody platform. Red used his rifle like a battering ram, and Sonny relied on his strength to push them back to the edge and over. Some were coming up the stairs, charging the front door. Boom! It was Pete's shotgun. *Good! He was still alive.* And boom again! The blasts came so close together that the two Renaissance bounced off each other in midair as they flew back down the steps.

Some of those at the steps who had made it to the platform were riddled with Sonny's fire when he broke free and turned to meet their challenge. Mike Looney climbed through the window and fired at some stragglers retreating from the steps. Red struggled with the two that were left. No, three. Here comes one after me. I pressed on my trigger and nothing happened. It was jammed. I swung the rifle around and flung it butt first into his face. He reeled backward and then raised his AR15 to his bloody face. The side of his head blew apart together with his rifle, splattering bloody metal fragments across the doorway. *Damn!*

An M16 started firing behind me! I spun around and saw Sam firing into the rear of the storeroom. And then I saw the human shapes in the darkness. They must have climbed through the opening in the destroyed wall.

"Behind us!" I yelled. I felt vulnerable without a weapon and turned to the door of the dorm room just as Pat Looney came running out. He tossed me an M16 with his good arm and then pulled a .38-caliber pistol from his pocket. We both turned and opened fire in support of Sam.

The firing from the rear of the storeroom was light, but combined with the rooftop cover fire, it made us bunch together at the loading doorway, first back to back but before long all facing into the storeroom. Then, almost as though a switch had been thrown to activate special event lighting, flashes of small blasts began to leap across the dark. The AR15s were blowing up, just like the one that could have done me in. And like the Renaissance soldier who tried to do me in, there were no screams of pain. It was quick and the shock so sudden that they were dead before they knew why.

The M60 opened fire again, and I associated it with Johnny, relieved to know he was back in action. "There's explosions on the rooftop," he yelled, confirming his health.

A volley of shots rang out, and I could see about a dozen troops charging at us from the damaged storeroom. I don't know if we had let down our guard in awe and anticipation of the rigged guns finally destroying themselves, but the charging Renaissance were only about twenty feet away before we raised our weapons again. Pat Looney was standing a few feet in front of me when he ran out of ammo and hurled his pistol toward the rushing troops. He was bent forward in a pitcher's release stance when the back of his head blew out like a coconut shell bursting open. Blood and brains splattered across the side of my face, and I stared in disbelief at his body falling to the floor.

The rifle fire was suddenly mute, muffled from my existence. I heard nothing and could only see Pat on the floor. The battle was over. *I quit!*

"Grenade!"

I was hearing words that I had heard only a short time ago. Maybe I was reliving the battle, trying to go back a few minutes in time so Pat would still be alive. No, he was there on the floor. I could see him. But I remembered Sam saying that they only had one grenade. *So, I must be hallucinating. There couldn't be another grenade.*

The explosion knocked someone into me. I found myself flying backward and slamming into the wall between the doors. I didn't know if I had dropped my rifle in surrender or if it had now been dislodged from my grip, but I found myself sitting empty-handed on the floor, leaning against the wall with Sam lying in front of me. His face was covered with deep red punctures, and the front of his body and clothing were shredded. There was loud gunfire around me again. The self-imposed unconscious respite was over.

I looked past Sam and saw someone in a vest carrying an AK47 fall and slide forward. He came to a stop inches from Sam, his weapon somewhere behind him, and lifted a clenched fist. His arm trembled in an effort to thrust forward. "Lousy traitor!" he rasped, and his fist fell with a meaty slap onto the concrete near Sam's head. Then there were people standing in front of us. I couldn't see their faces. Did they break through our defense? I either couldn't or didn't want to raise my head to look at them. The hell with everything, it's over.

"I guess I was wrong," Sam said in a loud whisper, spitting blood over his matted beard. "I thought they only had one. Or maybe they found one that I left behind back there." He chuckled, and there was a gurgle in his throat. "Funny but, either way, I guess I did it...I did it to myself." His head rolled away from me and he was silent.

Someone helped me to my feet. "Jim! Jim, are you OK?" It was Pete. He was leading me to the dorm room. I stumbled on the ever-present shell casings at the entrance and wiped the side of my face with my sleeve. There was still something there. I held my cuff and wiped harder, rubbed until my temple and cheek and ear were numb, until I couldn't feel anything sticky on my skin.

There was gunfire outside. *I was wrong. I couldn't get away. The battle was still going on.* I was inside the dorm room, and I saw Johnny sitting behind the M60. Both he and Pete were talking to me, but I couldn't understand what they were saying. I looked through the window frame and saw Red and Sonny. And I could hear Mike shouting and crying out and sobbing over his brother behind me. *When in God's name would this be over?*

"Are they gone?" I asked Pete.

"Who?"

"Are they gone from back there?" I pointed to the storeroom.

"Yeah," Pete said. "We got them all. But there's still more out front."

"Well, let's get them then," I said. "We have to get them and get the hell out of this fucking evil place. I need a gun. I keep losing my gun like the generals in the Civil War kept getting their horses shot out from under them."

Pete walked over to Johnny and took the M16 leaning against the wall near him. He loaded it with a fresh magazine. "That's the last clip I had on me," he said. "We sure used a ton of ammo."

"Here." I took two magazines from my pocket. "These are my last. Take one back."

"Keep them," Pete said. He patted the stock of his shotgun. "I'll stick with my baby."

"You OK, Jim?" Johnny asked. "You look shook up. You sure that grenade didn't get a piece of you?"

"Only inside my head," I said. "What about you? When I didn't hear the M60 going, I thought something had happened to you."

"I had to change the barrel. It was glowing red-hot. A lot of good it did; I only have one ammo belt left, about a hundred rounds. Pete covered me with his shotgun while I changed the barrel. I couldn't find the glove, so I rolled up my jacket to use as padding. My jacket caught fire and I burned my hands, but I'll live."

"I wish that for all of us who are still left, that we live," I said. "Poor Mike. Maybe we should…"

"They're firing at us again," Johnny shouted.

"From where?" I asked as I followed Pete and climbed through the window frame. The platform was clear of bodies, and I saw them piled on the cobblestones in front of the platform and around the Buick.

"There, inside the headquarters building," Red shouted as he pointed across the yard. "They must have marshaled over there from the roof and the gate and through that fire door."

"Once more into the breach, dear friends, once more," I recited.

"I haven't heard one of your wisecracks for hours," Red said. "And you start your comeback tour with Shakespeare?"

It seemed like all the motorcycles started at once. The revving of the throttles and the pulsating waves of engine roar resonated around the courtyard. At first glance, the barricade at the far end of the yard looked like the fire was still smoldering, but then it was clear that it was clouds of exhaust smoke pouring into the air.

"And here comes the cavalry," I said. "But not to rescue *us.*"

"Is the key in the truck?" Red asked. "Maybe we can try to bust through the gate area now that no one is protecting it."

Key. Key. Me, I've got... "I've got the key," I said. I held it out for Red.

The key was snatched from my hand before Red could reach for it. Mike Looney jumped from the platform and used the M37 hood like a trampoline, reaching the ground in one bound.

"Those bastards will pay for what they did to my brother!" he shouted.

Before we could follow him, to stop him or help him, the troops in the headquarters building opened fire. We backed off and could only provide cover fire for Mike as he struggled to open the passenger door. He finally tossed his M16 into the cab through the window opening and followed it in. The engine started immediately and, as the truck backed away from the rear of the platform, I saw that the windshield had been blown out from previous gunfire. Johnny opened up with the M60 as we retreated to the rear of the platform.

There were a series of AR15 detonations across the yard, almost unnoticed over the drama of the M37 racing toward the rear of the yard and motorcycles weaving out from the sides of the barricade. Two Harleys zipped past the truck on either side and headed for us. The truck turned sharply when it reached the damaged section of the barricade and plowed its way behind the flimsy structure. Three more bikes pushed out the far side like they were water being displaced from a pool by the M37 diving into those behind them.

Mike had navigated through the staging area between the building and barricade, in forward and reverse, bouncing and crushing machines and riders under his tires with loud crunching noises, before the five that had escaped regrouped and reached us. We concentrated fire in their direction, downing three. One of their gas tanks exploded, and the two still rolling turned back.

There were two more AR15 detonations across the yard and then silence.

The M37 was under fire from the barracks as it ripped off the end of the barricade in turning out into the open courtyard. Still taking hits from behind, it accelerated toward the retreating motorcycles. It smashed into one, and the rider flew above the roofline and recoiled off the canvas top as his bike skidded out from under the front wheels. The second motorcycle crossed in front of the truck, circled, and returned at top speed like a charging knight in a joust, the rider steadying an AK47 on his handlebars. Mike turned to meet him. The rider and Mike exchanged gunfire while in each other's field of vision, and the biker lost. He hit the cobblestones and his cycle continued without him. It tore through the weakened barricade, crashed through a doorway, and exploded inside the barracks building, starting a new fire.

The M37 weaved erratically back across the courtyard and stopped near the headquarters building, about fifty feet from the pocket of Renaissance troops across from us. We couldn't see if Mike was injured or if he was just catching a breath.

"I'm out of ammo," Sonny said as he slammed his last magazine into his rifle.

"Me, too," I said.

Red walked into the storeroom and returned in less than a minute. "The box is empty. What we have is *it.*" He pulled four magazines from his pocket and handed them out. "Set your selectors on single shot. We can't afford to pour out automatic fire anymore. How you doing, Johnny?"

"Half a belt. That's it," Johnny said.

"OK, cover us and don't fire unless it's absolutely necessary," Red said. "I always believed that the best defense is a good offense, so let's take it to them and end this thing."

CHAPTER TWENTY-SEVEN

We followed Red down the steps and spread out as we walked slowly toward the headquarters building. With each step, I expected someone from somewhere to start shooting. We got closer, and nothing. I looked toward the barracks. The fire was devouring the flammable interior building materials, and I could smell the burning wood drifting on the shadows of smoke. I could still hear motorcycle engines running. I turned back. We were twenty feet away. Ten. We reached the building without incident. Red was the first through the door. "Clear," he shouted.

We followed Red in, and I saw that Lenny's body was still where I had left him. The others paused a moment to look at him, and I again promised to get him out of there. We were guided by two flashlights and went through the inside vestibule door to the rooms that branched out to the sides. There was no one at all but the dead, and we had killed none of them. They all had damaged AR15s lying nearby. There were undamaged rifles scattered around the area as well, dropped by those who finally realized that there was something terribly wrong with the weapons and who probably had come down from their high and decided it was time to leave.

We were getting ready to leave when one of the flashlight beams highlighted a body in the rear of the room. It was wearing a red vest and was balled up in a fetal position. We walked back to it and saw that the two-inch-thick gauze around the side of the Leader's head was bright red and so saturated with blood that streaks had run down his neck and along the features of his face.

"I guess they opened that fire door and he came down here with what was left of his troops to make a last stand," I said.

Red squatted to check the body. "There are no other wounds. He bled to death from his head wound."

"See that, Pete, you *were* the one that got him," I said. "It just took a little longer than you thought."

We stepped outside again and began walking toward the M37. Its headlights were off, but the engine was running and the growing fire at the barracks silhouetted the truck. Suddenly the horn began to blare. We thought it was a warning, and we all ducked back against the building.

"Mike," Red shouted. He waved his hand above his head. "There's none of them left down here. Get off the horn."

We reached the truck and Red pushed Mike back from the steering wheel. The horn stopped sounding. The cab of the truck was riddled with bullet holes, and so was Mike. He was dead. His M16 was still resting on the dash, poking out the windshield frame.

We removed Mike from the cab and carried his body to the empty bed. Our return cargo would be our dead.

The motorcycle engines that I had heard earlier roared louder. Two of them sped out the far end of the barricade and hugged the building line on the opposite side of the yard. The lead rider held a large white bedsheet aloft, and it streamed behind him. *They were surrendering?*

The second bike had a passenger and followed only a few feet behind the first. When the passenger saw us, he hurled his AR15 away and it bounced and shattered into pieces on the ground.

"They want out," Red said. "Should we let them…?"

Johnny fired a quick burst as the second bike crossed his sights and sent the passenger sailing halfway across the yard. The first Harley hit the barbed wire and the spikes of the downed gates, which blew out its tires and sent the rider into a launch, like a human cannonball, his machine somersaulting close behind. They disappeared across the road.

The second motorcycle was tilted at a forty-five-degree angle from the sudden shift of weight and hit the ground as it reached the gates. The operator rolled and tumbled, and then stopped abruptly as he became impaled on the barbed-wire spikes. The bedsheet truce flag fluttered to the ground and partially covered him.

"I guess that answers my question," Red said. "Come on, let's go get Lenny and head back to the room."

Lenny was placed in the truck bed next to Mike, and Red drove us back to the platform. We disassembled the machine gun and collected the empty crates, weapons, and personal baggage. We pulled the license plates from the Buick, and Pete volunteered to hike back to the shot-up Chevy to do the same. The cars could still be traced through the VIN numbers, but I had a feeling they may have been reported stolen along with the Peterbilt.

"Don't leave anything that shows U.S. Army on it," Red said. "We can't show that the army had any presence here."

We left room for the bodies of Pat and Sam among the freight and closed up the rear tailgate. I could smell the barracks fire more keenly now and looked back at it. The entire interior of the south end was ablaze, flames visible through its portals. It seemed to be confined to only the inside of the barracks and, because the exterior wall was brick, would probably burn itself out eventually. I wondered, though, if the town would consider organizing another bucket brigade or just let their monument to greed—and now war—be destroyed.

"You'll have to lift up the gate so I can drive through," Red was saying. "I don't want to take a chance on blowing a tire."

I came around to the front of the M37.

"Jim, you and Pete get the ends and I'll lift the middle," Sonny said. "After he drives through, we'll ease it back down."

I avoided looking at the biker impaled on the other gate as I lined up to lift the twisted section on the side near our room. We deposited our rifles on the ground.

Johnny, M-16 cradled in his arms, hands bandaged and not functional for this task, scouted around outside the wall. "It looks like most of the town is coming up the road, but I don't see any Renaissance with them. I'll keep an eye on them," he reported. "And I'll guide Red around the obstacles out here."

"On three," Sonny instructed. We squatted and grabbed hold of what had been the vertical lock support of the iron gate. "One…Two…Three."

The gate lifted and we walked it back, raising it as we moved our hands to another bar or two at a time and finally pressing it against the brick wall and post. It was heavy, and I didn't think I could hold it up for long. *Let's go, Red. We all aren't muscle-bound like Sonny.*

Red maneuvered the M37 past us and gave a nudge to the overturned van to clear it out of the way. Once we saw he was clear and on the road, we started walking the gate back down. We got it to waist height when Sonny switched the position of his hands and told us to back off. We gladly complied, and the muscle man eased the section to the ground by himself.

"I don't want somebody to get a hernia after surviving all we went through," Sonny said as he turned to us. "To tell you the truth, there were times that I didn't think I would survive."

A pistol shot rang out from behind us, and a red splotch blossomed out of Sonny's chest.

"Take that, you bastard," Martha screamed from behind us. "That's what you deserved in the first place."

We scrambled for our weapons as Martha fired another shot. Sonny stood rigid and straight for a moment. His body had absorbed the impact of the two bullets but now toppled backward, and the gate rattled from his fall.

Pete had found his shotgun and fired at the platform where Martha stood, half hidden in the shadows. She disappeared without as much as a whimper, and the only sound was her pistol clattering along the cement. Then, in some sort of death twitch, her bare foot jerked in and out of the dark before it rested over the edge of the platform.

Two dozen townspeople appeared from around the far post. They glanced at Sonny, who was huddled over by Red and Johnny. A white straw hat appeared in the crowd, and someone pushed his way to the front.

"Oh, no, don't tell me it was her," Martha's brother shouted. "I told her to forget about him, to not come back." He looked around the area, saw Martha's foot, and climbed onto the platform. As soon as he slipped into the darkness, he let out a cry. "Oh, no. No. She's dead. You killed her." He reappeared on the edge of the platform. "What is wrong with you people? Haven't you killed enough without wanting more and more bloodshed? Must you kill everyone and everything that crosses your path?"

The crowd had tripled in size and began to murmur, spurred on by the brother's mournful words.

"Why don't you murderers go back where you came from?" they shouted.

"Get out of here and leave us in peace, you bloodthirsty animals!"

"But she killed…" Pete turned to look at Sonny. Red's expression confirmed that Sonny was dead. "But, she shot and killed Sonny out of ambush, for no reason," Pete said as he turned back to the crowd.

"You didn't have to kill her!" the brother shouted again. "Get out!"

"Get out! Get out! Get out!" the chant went up.

"You ungrateful bastards," Pete yelled. "Don't you know what we did for you? How can you…?"

"Save your breath, Pete," I said. "You'll never convince them that we're not the bad guys. Let's get out of here."

They continued the chant as we loaded Sonny's body onto the truck, and it rang in our ears as we drove off. The truck was pelted with stones as a parting tribute.

CHAPTER TWENTY-EIGHT

None of us wanted to ride in the bed, to be sitting in the dark with the bodies of friends, so all four squeezed into the cab. I sat in the shotgun seat and Pete sat sideways on my knees, leaning his arm into the open windshield frame.

The first two posts along the road were deserted. I couldn't even tell where they had been and only knew they had been somewhere along this road from seeing them earlier. The last, the so-called doomsday post, was marked by a foot-deep crater the width of the road and ten feet in circumference. The headlights shone on the twisted skeleton of a car tossed to the side of the road and its scattered body parts strewn about. The legs of several bodies were sticking out of the woods. We stopped to survey the scene. We had only been on the road for ten minutes, but I was glad to get a break from the cramped seating arrangements.

We couldn't tell what had actually happened but surmised that there had been an altercation and then a deliberate detonation of a bomb buried under the road. That was why it was probably named the doomsday post, the last resort being to blow up everyone, attacker and defender, as a final desperate act. All of the bodies we could see were Renaissance soldiers. We guessed that when the discipline had broken down, factions had fought among themselves, one trying to leave and the other trying to prevent desertion. The vehicle that had been blown up was not the false sarin truck, so we were fairly sure it had passed through here and reached the body shop for repainting.

Red moved the M37 slowly forward, sinking slightly into the blast hole, and then emerged on the other side. We boarded again and intersected with a black-top one-lane road in about another half mile. Red turned onto the road and seemed to know the way to the contact point, probably from directions given to him by Sam. The road was unlit and continued on and on into the night, weaving through curves and up and down the sides of mountains. We shivered from the night air whipping through the windshield opening and only raised our heads to squint ahead when the truck slowed and the wind wouldn't bring tears to our eyes. Red had found a pair of goggles in a compartment under the dash, so he was able to see where he was going. We stopped twice to stretch our legs, water the trees, and change seating positions.

Someone finally found the heater under our bench seat and turned it on. At least it kept our lower extremities warm. We cheered once when, after an hour into the trip, a car passed us heading in the opposite direction. It was the only sign of life we had seen since our departure from the Nirvana Valley. If there was any concern with being stopped by some branch of law enforcement, it didn't seem to bother Red.

Dawn was beginning to peek from behind the mountains in the east when we reached the town. I didn't see the name on the small sign and didn't really care. I was glad to be anywhere that even hinted of civilization. Red guided the truck down the one-block main street and turned at the last building, a long white cinder block structure with a faded red gas pump in front. He parked at a double garage door, and we all slipped sorely and gingerly out of the truck.

Red knocked on the upper frosted glass of an entry door at the side of the garage doors, and a light turned on inside within seconds. The tall, thin man who opened the door was wearing gray, dried grease–smudged coveralls with a cloth name tag—Arthur—in blue letters. Red showed him two credential cases, one of which I had seen Sam give him, and after the man opened both and looked us over, we were told to enter. He was apparently Sam's contact.

The sweet biting odor of freshly sprayed paint wafted through the building and was strongest when we stopped outside the open room with crude lettering across its header that read PAINT SHOP. The light was sparse, but we could see through the wide doorway that two Renaissance men were sitting on wooden chairs next to the shiny black M37, their backs to the doorway. Their AK47s were leaning against the air compressor used to power paint sprayers, and our weapons had been left in the bed of our truck. Arthur waved us back into the hall, walked over to a metal toolbox on a trolley, and opened the lid.

"The others are here," Arthur announced with a Midwest twang as he reached for a wall switch behind the tool trolley.

The two Renaissance men turned without rising. With a sudden loud whine, the air compressor churned on and the two toppled back, twisting and hitting the dirt floor, a red dot on each of their foreheads. Arthur held a smoking .38-caliber revolver. He turned to us and beckoned us into the room.

"How are you gonna explain them?" Red asked after Arthur turned off the compressor.

"Sons of bitches tried to rob me," Arthur said. "I have a very good rapport with the local sheriff, and the state police will be notified by the bureau's local field office. So where's Sam?"

We all looked at the floor; then Red said, "His body is in the back of our truck."

Arthur reached back and flipped on the air compressor switch. He walked over to the two dead Renaissance and emptied the remainder of his bullets into them, came back to the switch, and returned the room to silence.

We were all silent for a few minutes, staring at the two and then at Arthur, who was nonchalantly going about the business of removing the masking tape and paper from the windows of the M37. No one was stunned or compassionate in any way over Arthur's actions.

"OK, I have calls to make," Red finally said. "Do you have a secure line?"

"Yeah, up front in the office," Arthur answered. "The one on the desk goes through the town switchboard, but I have a private line in the desk drawer."

"I've got calls to make after you," Johnny said.

"I can wait my turn," Arthur said.

We spent the next hour tidying up, filling in Arthur on most of what had happened, showering and shaving in yet another hole-in-the-wall bathroom, moving the two Renaissance to the office and staging their bodies to look like they had tried to stick up the place, and moving our M37 into the garage—where Arthur viewed Sam's body and cursed—before finally sitting down to steaming hot coffee from Arthur's stainless steel urn. Johnny's burned hands were treated by Arthur's expert first aid. The phone calls had been made, and wheels had been set in motion by several sources. One of those sources had a haberdasher from another town deliver a van full of clothes, shoes, and accessories in all sizes so we could each choose a complete new outfit from the lot. We were slowly acclimating back into the real world.

CHAPTER TWENTY-NINE

The second vehicle of the many that would be visiting Arthur's Garage and Body Shop that day arrived a half hour after the final phone call had been made. It was a limo, and it was our transportation home.

"But, what about Lenny and the others?" I asked when I found that we survivors would end this adventure in luxury.

"They'll be taken care of. Arrangements have been made," Johnny said. "We'll see them again as soon as we can."

It was time to leave before the sheriff or state police arrived and wondered what we had to do with the stickup and deaths of the thieves. Everyone's personal gear was loaded into the trunk of the limo, and we all lined up in the garage to say good-bye to Arthur.

"This is yours," Red said. He handed Sam's credential case to Arthur, and I saw that it was Sam's ID and badge. I only caught a glimpse of the picture, but it was Sam without his beard and long hair, not at all recognizable as Snark. Sam had retrieved it from wherever he had hidden it for that year of undercover and trusted it to Red, maybe having a premonition of his death or knowing he didn't have to worry about it getting into the wrong hands and hurting his career.

"He was a good man," Arthur said. "Thanks for getting his remains out of there so we can give him his proper honors."

"They were all good men," Red said. "Ours will be picked up within the hour. Thanks for looking out for them until then."

"Maybe we'll all get a chance to work together again someday," Arthur said. "It would be my pleasure."

We climbed into the back of the limo, and when the doors were closed and the tinted windows and front privacy glass separating us from the driver comfortably surrounded us, I asked, "Who were we supposed to be?"

"Top secret," Red said. "Arthur was told in one of many of our phone calls that we were formed as a secret elite unit with the highest priority. Everything has been taken care of at every level."

There were bags of hot bacon and egg sandwiches and coffee and Danishes waiting for us. I hadn't realized how hungry I was until I took the first bite. I sat in the jump seat and the others on the long black leather bench seat. As we started out of town, the sheriff's car and a black hearse with CORONER'S OFFICE in white letters on the driver's door passed us. How many trips would that second vehicle have to make today? More than it probably had for the past two years combined. Just make sure you take care of our boys. Get them home to us.

After we ate, the weariness and fatigue overcame everyone, and the comfort of the soft leather seats enticed us into a much-needed sleep. The conversations gradually died out, and the compartment became a luxury flophouse resonating with the snores of deep slumber.

I was the last to awake. Everyone was holding a drink glass and was smiling. There was soft music drifting from hidden speakers.

"What'll you have?" Johnny asked.

"Vodka and seven would be nice." I rubbed my eyes and squinted through the tinted glass. "Where are we?"

"About a hundred miles north of the city," Johnny said. "Frank, the driver, had to find another route. The throughway is gridlocked with traffic."

I took a sip of the drink Pete had mixed and smiled when I thought of what I had said to Gwen about her friends only buying things that came from communist countries. Here I was consuming the Soviet Union's national drink. I guess I was also a hypocrite, as I had called them. But hell, I now knew that almost everyone is. It's hard to stay on a steady path of commitment to an ideal. I guess that's why Clarence and Martha's brother and the rest became hermits, so they didn't have to compromise, so they could follow that one-track railroad and be content that there was a track.

The sleep had cleared my head, and I thought of Gwen again. If I had to compromise in my life, it would be to Gwen. Now that I had survived my awakening and had expunged my soul of any further wants or needs to prove myself, I would focus on her and our future together. The differences in how we feel about which course the country should follow is like the differences in a relationship. It takes both ends of the spectrum and both partners to make it work.

"Do we pass Poughkeepsie?" I asked.

"We can pass anywhere we want," Johnny said.

"Would you mind if I got off there and caught up with you guys in a day or two?"

"I don't know," Red said. "I'll have to find out if you guys are allowed to contact anyone outside those involved before being debriefed."

"Debriefed?" I said. "By who?"

"My unit. It's part of our deal."

"Whose deal?" I asked.

"Look, Jim," Johnny interrupted, "we agreed to cooperate on certain things in order to put this deal together."

"So I can't visit my girl until the army says so?" I asked.

"It's not like that," Johnny said. "Come on, Red, you know he won't say anything." He turned back to me. "Would you?"

I shook my head. "I never have before. You really don't think someone would believe this fantastic story even if I did tell it, do you?"

"He wasn't on the original roster, and even if they find out he was there, he could've been missing in action for a couple of days," Johnny said. "Then happened to show up back home."

Red looked at the floor, contemplating the situation. "Yeah, I guess that would work," he finally said. He pointed his index finger at me. "But not a word, understand? They would come down very hard on you."

"You think they scare me after what we've just gone through? If people in government would stop threatening everyone and try a different approach, maybe they'd get some cooperation." I saw Red getting nervous about my attitude. "I swear by God and the code of the Vandals to never reveal what happened," I said, holding up the palm of my hand. "And you know there's no higher oath than that."

Red smiled. "OK. When your MIA status is up, check into the club."

I looked at Johnny.

"Yeah, Kelly told me on the phone that you're welcome anytime," Johnny said.

Pete leaned forward, pressed a button to partially open the privacy glass, and spoke in a low voice to the driver. He closed the panel and leaned back. "Next stop, Poughkeepsie," he said.

"You're gonna need some cash for a change of clothes and walking-around money," Johnny said. He reached into his pants pocket.

"I still have that hundred," I said. I patted the upper pocket of my new sport jacket.

Johnny shoved some bills into the pocket. "Magic! It just tripled, like rabbits. And when we see you at home, we'll talk about what you earned today."

I would've protested in the past, become nervous over accepting what could be considered illicit money, or flat out refused. But maybe Lenny had been right and I should stop being a sucker. Like Johnny said, I earned it. I helped take it away from a bunch of scumbags, so why not share in it, if even just a little piece?

"By the way, I didn't see the suitcase with the money being loaded from the room or into the trunk," I said.

"Well, when we get it home, it'll have to be laundered," Johnny said. "Because it was divided up among everybody's dirty wash in our bags."

"Red, do you think those guys had a chance of succeeding with their plan?" I asked.

"Not even if they were delivered the real stuff," Red said. "Their leadership had the military ability of agitators at a mob scene. All they would've accomplished was to hurt and kill a lot of innocent people before they were crushed."

"So, I guess we still accomplish a noble deed after all."

"We weren't there to be noble," Johnny said. "We were there for vengeance and to pull a scam on a bunch of idiots who, in their warped minds, thought *they* were about to do a noble deed. We accomplished both, with a lot more difficulty and loss than planned, but still done. I didn't see you tossing down the bills I just put in your pocket like you did with the first hundred. That's because you're beginning to realize that there's no such thing as a purely noble cause. There's always monetary gain as the ultimate goal, no matter how much BS is smeared on the surface. Money means power to do what you want. The world runs on money and always will. Those that don't grasp that will never be capable of completing their noble cause, because they won't have money to back them up."

"I kind of feel that way but with exceptions," Red said. "I spent two tours in Nam, and I can tell you that the arrogance of the top brass in underestimating the enemy and thinking our superior numbers and technology will eventually win are what will make this thing drag on and on. But I'm still passionate for the noble cause part of it, for making sure my men have a chance to get home in one piece, and for my country. I took an oath and I feel the commitment in here." Red tapped on his chest and smiled. "And, if you call army pay the power of money behind my noble cause, Johnny, you're off by a wide margin."

"Yes, but wasn't it backup money that started this little adventure and the promise of a big payoff before the army even became involved?" Johnny added with his own knowing smile.

"Well, you guys can philosophize all you want," Pete said, "but, as far as I'm concerned, I rid the world of some cruddy little bastard who had no purpose in life but to hurt and kill people. That's my contribution, noble or not. Now my mom can rest in peace."

"Here, here."

"What's scary is that no one will ever know what could've happened," I said. "And someday in the future, some of these arrogant little shits that have no idea what they survived will grow up to become arrogant politicians. Can you imagine us having a draft dodger as president some day?"

"They would probably get rid of the draft."

"Or have sex parties in the White House."

We all laughed and had another drink.

Red had carried a small toiletry case into the limo with him. He lifted it off the seat and unzipped it. "I was going to give these out later, but since Jim will be getting off soon, I'll do it now."

He pulled out three long, narrow cases and opened one. Inside was a medal attached to a red ribbon with a center yellow stripe. "This is the National Defense Medal," Red said. "It's given to military personnel who serve in time of war. If you were in the military, you would be eligible for a much higher award for what you did today, but consider this a token of my grateful thanks for what we did— for that noble cause part of our mission. My gift to you."

Red handed Johnny and Pete their cases. He opened the other. "Jim, since you were probably already awarded one of these when you served, I'm going to hold on to it until I can get and attach a device indicating a second award." He shook all our hands. "Thank you all for defending our nation, no matter what purpose you say you were here for."

They inspected their awards, and I felt in awe because I knew that this gift came straight from Red's heart and it would be a remembrance of all our camaraderie and the sacrifice of our friends.

A newsbreak had replaced the background music on the radio, and the next story perked all our ears.

"…mechanical malfunction accidentally caused a series of rockets to fire while the helicopter was on a flight to a live fire training exercise at Fort Drum in upstate New York. The rockets struck and completely destroyed an abandoned factory complex. The area is extremely remote and mostly uninhabited except for a nearby isolated commune. Units of both the military and local state police investigated the incident, saying that the rubble of the buildings completely buried everything inside. There were no reported injuries and the matter is considered closed…"

Everyone looked at Red, and I knew it was one of the phone calls he had made that had activated this *mechanical malfunction.*

"I guess that takes care of Fortress Renaissance and all its secrets," he said. He held up his glass in a toast. "Here's to the National Guard."

CHAPTER THIRTY

The week that followed was hectic. I had waited for Gwen in the hotel lobby and, when she and her cast had returned, found that because of the heavy traffic in the area, they didn't come within ten miles of the Woodstock festival before having to turn around and come back. I spent the next two days with Gwen and frequently exchanged pleasantries with her friends, completely avoiding any political debates or discussions.

Gwen told me several times that she saw a change in me. I couldn't tell her what had caused that change and only hinted that I was trying to change my attitude so we could become closer. I still held most of my patriotic views, but in somewhat tempered form. I was sure that time would eventually put this era of national division into the history books and allow us, as through most of history, a sometimes bumpy road but always the hope for a brighter future.

I became a frequent visitor at Benny's club where Johnny and Pete had chastised me before our adventure. I heard from Johnny and Pete that Red or his superiors didn't need to see me after all, but Red did leave my medal for me before he left. The army had awarded him his own medal, and he was now wearing captain's bars for real. He was off on another assignment, parts unknown. He didn't know it then, but bearer bonds with high-yield maturities had been purchased and locked away in a safe deposit box in his name. His friends felt that his eventual meager retirement pay could use a supplemental boost and that maybe, by that time; he would get over being noble.

Knowing I had taken a solemn vow of silence, Johnny and Pete had told me some of the background of the aftermath. Arthur had taken care of disposing of the M37s and everything connected with them. His shop had been closed and he, too, was off on another assignment. None of the other civilian vehicles were ever found, and I was never the adjuster on their subsequent claims.

About a third of the Renaissance loot had been used to make the incident less and less likely to have happened.

The coroner had been convinced that the deaths of our four friends were the result of an auto accident that occurred while they had been on a local hunting trip. With death certificates filed, the bodies were released to a funeral home in a nearby town that was owned by the cousin of the owner of the funeral home in our neighborhood. After the bodies were transported back home, the best cosmetologists were brought in to hide any traces of gunshot wounds so the families would believe their accidental deaths and could have an open-casket wake. The families had been surprised to know that each of their loved ones had a life insurance policy for a substantial amount of money, with their next of kin as beneficiary.

I still led my straight life, but with a few perks. No one around the club was ever told about our adventure, but all had some vague ideas that the auto accident and the raised status of the survivors of the trip were for a definite reason. I never paid for anything within the walls of the club—not for drinks, food, bowling games, or pool games. The bartender even gave me quarters for the jukebox anytime I wanted to hear some music. I was an inexplicable hero and no one had to know why, especially not from me. Last, but most engaging for me, was that I bought Lenny's Cadillac from his family with some of my "bonus" money so I could park my ass on those leather seats and be reminded of him telling me not to be a sucker in this life.

I went to all three funerals—Pat and Mike Looney being buried together—and to the wakes beforehand. It was a season of wakes and funerals that we were all happy to have finally ended. Each of their coffins mysteriously displayed a long and narrow open case housing a red and yellow ribbon and medal. No one but we survivors knew they had been placed there to honor our friends for their defense of our nation.

THE END

978-0-595-39098-4
0-595-39098-6

Printed in the United States
53574LVS00007B/1-51

9 780595 390984